Scarlet Yearnings

BEYOND FIRST GLANCE

Scarlet Ibis James

TRADE EDITION

BY SCARLET IBIS JAMES

Scarlet Yearnings

BEYOND FIRST GLANCE

Scarlet Ibis James

Edited by D. James Joseph

DKJ Enterprises LLC

Scarlet Yearnings Beyond First Glance

Published by DKJ Enterprises LLC, United States

Publication Date: June 1, 2026

The characters portrayed in this book are entirely fictitious, each with its own unique story. Any similarity to actual persons, living or dead, is purely coincidental and not intended by the author.

James Baldwin, excerpt from "Down at the Cross" from The Fire Next Time. Originally published in The New Yorker (November 9, 1962) as "Letter from a Region in My Mind." Copyright © 1962, 1963 by James Baldwin, renewed 1991, 1992 by Gloria Baldwin Karefa-Smart. Reprinted with permission of The Permissions Company LLC on behalf of the James Baldwin Estate.

BOOK TEAM: Development Editor: D. James Joseph | Proofreader: Alice Heritage | **Cover Design, Trade Edition: 100Covers.com** | Cover Design, Collector's Edition: Nick Low | Beta Readers: Luna Bridges, Badiana Badio Eckstrom, LuAnn James, and Margo Thomas.

For information, please email the publisher at publisher@dkj-e.com

Trade Edition (Illustrated Cover):
eBook ISBN: 979-8-9915909-4-5
Paperback: ISBN: 979-8-9993829-3-1
Hardcover: ISBN: 979-8-9993829-4-8

Collector's Edition (Narrative Art Cover):
Paperback: ISBN: 979-8-9993829-6-2
Hardcover: ISBN: 979-8-9993829-5-5

LCCN #2025925575 (print)

https://scarletibisjames.com/

I dedicate this collection of short stories to those of us who know and who will discover that love beyond first glance isn't magic, it's maintenance . . . and absolutely worth it.

Contents

Foreword

I thought I had told it all. When I wrote *Scarlet Yearnings*, I believed I had emptied the well. That debut collection, published independently, featured twelve stories that bared my soul, each reflecting a longing I had carried for years. I didn't expect anyone to ask, "But what happened after?"

And yet, you did.

Readers wanted more of the lives I had briefly opened and then left suspended. You were eager to hear from the men, the partners, the mothers, and the neighbors. You wanted to see what love looks like after the curtain falls, expose what "happily ever after" means in real life, when desire has done its dazzling work and the reckoning begins.

I initially returned to the opening story, "The First Time She Met Her Father," intending to write a simple continuation. What emerged instead was something truer and harder: emotional autobiographical fiction that refused to remain a short story. That literary and spirit-filled work became my second book, *Scarlet Birthright: What They Left Behind*.

Now, I continue my response to your original request. *Scarlet Yearnings Beyond First Glance* revisits many of those earlier stories, sometimes through a fresh pair of eyes and sometimes by stepping into the "after" only hinted at before. Some threads unravel, others weave into surprising new patterns, and a few fray at the edges in ways that startled even me. To complete the circle of twelve, I've also added new voices that echo, challenge, and harmonize with the originals. This collection explores love in all its forms—from the halls of a hospital to the far reaches of the cosmos.

It is important to note that while these stories share a lineage, the collection in *Beyond First Glance* stands entirely on its own. In fact, every book in this series is a standalone read; there is no requirement to have read *Scarlet Yearnings* or *Scarlet Birthright* in a particular order. Your way is the divine way through all these pages.

If *Scarlet Yearnings: Stories of Love and Desire* was about the ache of desire, *Scarlet Yearnings Beyond First Glance* is about love's reckoning: what it means to stay, to leave, to return, or to reimagine. Love isn't always gentler the second time. It can be sharper and more demanding, but it is also truer.

This book exists because of you, my readers. Your curiosity pulled me back to the page, forced me to listen to the silences I had left behind, and reminded me that stories, like relationships, deserve second glances. I offer you these twelve tales as both a continuation and a confession, for those who know that love rarely ends with the first look. It deepens, falters, reawakens, and eventually finds its authentic form.

—Scarlet Ibis James

Foreword

Released for the Day

The voice hits her first.

Nadine is standing in the line that snakes along the hallway of the courthouse, clutching her jury summons and her stainless steel coffee cup, half listening to the clerk's instructions. The fluorescent lights buzz. Someone's baby fusses. A man in front of her keeps shifting his weight like the floor is lava.

Behind her, someone laughs. A deep, rough-edged sound, the same pitch she remembers catching across a library table all those years ago.

She feels it in her ribs before her brain catches up.

"Yeah, they had me here last month, man," the voice says. "They lost my paperwork, called me again. I thought it was a prank."

Her coffee suddenly tastes like nothing. Her hands go numb.

It cannot be.

She tells herself that a lot of Black men have voices like that. Warm, a little rough at the edges, carrying music even in complaint. She tells herself she is being ridiculous, romantic, old and in need of . . .

Then he says, "You know how they do," with that exact sly dip in tone on "You know," and the hallway dissolves.

Twenty-two years fall away. The cold of a London winter. The smell of instant coffee and paper in the student library. His head tipped back as he laughed at something she said. The way his consonants curled around her name.

Nadine.

Her heart is beating too fast. She is forty-four years old, a manager at a nonprofit, the person everyone calls when they need a calm brain. She is wearing her sensible dark blue tweed blazer. Her curls are pinned up, scattered with a few betraying silvers. She is not the girl who used to twist her hair with ballpoint pens on study breaks.

She is about to turn around.

The clerk calls out, "If your last name begins with J through M, please follow the officer to the right."

Nadine's legs stay rooted.

"Miss?" the clerk says, closer now. "Ma'am, J through M."

Her body moves. She steps out of line, heart banging, and turns.

He is two people behind where she had been, mid-sentence to a woman in a floral mask. For half a second, she sees only what time has done. His hair is shorter, cropped close with threads of gray at the temples. His jaw is fuller. The boyishness has settled into something steadier.

Then he glances up, scanning the room, and their eyes meet.

It is like opening a book at the line you underlined years ago and finding it fresh and familiar all at once.

He blinks. His mouth pauses just a fraction. The woman next to him keeps talking, unaware, but his gaze stays on Nadine. Question, recognition, something like shock.

She feels her lips move into a slow smile that feels too big for her face.

"Charles?" she says, almost whispering.

The woman beside him stops. Charles turns fully now, and she hears, "Nadine?"

His accent has shifted, softened by years in America, but her name in his mouth is exactly as she remembers.

The clerk at the front is still calling letters. People are muttering and shuffling around them. Nadine steps aside so the line can move, never taking her eyes off him.

He laughs under his breath, a disbelieving sound. "Give me a few minutes," he says to the woman, then slips out of the line and walks toward Nadine.

It is not cinematic. There is no slow motion, no background score. His right shoe squeaks awkwardly on the linoleum. She almost snorts.

He stops an arm's length away, that careful distance people leave when they are not sure if they are allowed to touch you.

"Oh my God," he says. "It is you."

"Last I checked," she answers. "I am me."

They both laugh, a little brittle with nerves.

"You look . . ." He searches for a word, hand hovering in the air as if shaping it. "You look well."

That is such an adult thing to say that she wants to roll her eyes. "You look tired," she says, because honesty pops out of her when she is overwhelmed. Then quickly, "But in a good way. Like you sleep. Like you do your laundry on time."

He smiles properly now, the smile she remembers, crooked and cute. "I am deeply offended and strangely flattered."

Their letters are being called. Nadine's group is already filing through security.

"We are going to get yelled at," she says, glancing at the officer near the metal detector.

Charles follows her look, then pulls his phone from his pocket. "Can I take your number? Or give you mine. I am not losing you to the New York State Unified Court System."

She laughs and hears someone in line huff impatiently. They exchange numbers quickly, fingers fumbling, and then there is no more time.

As she walks away, she hears him tell the woman he had been talking to, "Sorry. That is someone I knew in another life."

Another life, she thinks, the metal detector arch framing her like a doorway. *Yes. Exactly that.*

***

Jury duty is a blur. A judge explains civic responsibilities. Lawyers ask strangers about bias. Nadine finds herself staring at one man's tie and remembering the fold of Charles's scarf around his neck in January of 2003. She gets released for the day before lunch. She walks out into bright downtown sunlight, free for the day, feeling unmoored.

Her phone buzzes.

Unknown number: "If this is Nadine from London, please confirm I am not hallucinating."

She laughs, standing at the corner of Jay Street and something she does not register.

"Yes, this is Nadine from London, currently on Jay Street, you are not hallucinating," she writes back.

Three dots. Then: "Can you do coffee? I am still trapped here, but they might dismiss for good behavior in an hour."

She hesitates only long enough to picture the emails she could catch up on, the laundry she meant to fold.

"Sure," she types. "There is a café on the corner of Court and Livingston. Text when you are out."

Her thumb hovers. Then she adds, without overthinking it, "I would like to see you."

She slips the phone into her bag and lets herself feel how true that is.

***

He arrives ninety minutes later, breathless, coat open to the February air. The bell over the café door jingles. Nadine looks up from her laptop, and there he is, framed by the window.

The years sit on him in a way she respects. His face is more angular, his shoulders broader. He wears a simple wool coat, a patterned scarf, and the same small gold ring in his left ear he had in his twenties. His skin, still the color of tamarind shell, looks deliberately cared for. The hair at his temples is gray, but his eyes, when they find her, are exactly the same, deep, piercing, yet with a kind of soft amusement.

She closes the laptop and stands.

"Hey," he says.

"Hey," she answers.

They hug. It is hesitant at first, a polite squeeze, but then his hand settles at the small of her back, and she breathes in familiar things: a lingering hint of shea butter, clean cotton, the ghosts of a younger man

______

8

who stayed up too late studying and working and still made time to listen to her talk.

When they pull apart, she sees there is something careful in his posture, like he does not want to rush this.

"You are real," he says.

"So are you," she says. "Which I am still processing."

They get coffee.

"So you live in Brooklyn," he says, stirring sugar into his cup. "That is what Google told me after I put your number in."

"You Googled me?" she laughs.

"Of course. I am a modern man. I'd like to know if the love of my youth is secretly a criminal."

Her spoon clinks against porcelain and goes still. *The love of my youth.* She feels the words land in the space between them, heavier than the joke he tries to make of it.

She looks up. He looks immediately sheepish.

"Too much?" he asks.

"Interesting," she says in an introspective tone.

There is a small silence. Around them, the café energy carries on. Someone's laptop dings with an email. A couple argues softly over a pastry.

He looks down at his coffee. "So. Tell me. Catch me up, Nadine from London."

She gives him the short version. Reminds him that she was from Trinidad and Tobago and had gotten a scholarship to London. Recalls the chaos of that year abroad when they met. Returning, finishing school, moving again for grad studies. Nonprofit work, one underpaying job after another, building a life in New York, one cramped apartment at a time. Eventually, a promotion, then another. A small but bright one-bedroom in Bed-Stuy that felt like home for the first time in a long time.

He listens the way she remembered, his focus a tangible thing.

"And romance?" he asks lightly, but in his voice, she hears a tension.

She lifts her shoulders up and drops them. "I dated. Cohabited once. We tried to assemble furniture without breaking up, failed, and broke up."

He laughs; she thinks it sounds like a low chord on an old guitar. "Nothing stuck," she continues. "I got good at taking care of myself. It became a habit."

"And now?"

"Now I am very competent, and my mother is still asking where her grandchildren are," she says. "What about you?"

He grimaces. "My mother is asking that in a louder register."

He sketches his life, filling in for what she missed. His return to Ghana when his father got sick. Years where his twenties blurred into hospital visits and side hustles, remittances and visa applications. The job in London that he did not take. The job in New York that he finally did. The consulting work that led to a stable position. Gradual stability, like a ladder with some missing rungs that he learned to climb anyway.

"No marriage," he says. "No kids. A few long relationships. Most ended when the weight of my obligations met the weight of their expectations."

"Is that what happened back then?" she asks, before she can stop herself. "With us."

His eyes flash to hers. It is suddenly quieter. It is a small café, but it feels like only the two of them are in it.

He takes a breath.

"That is a larger answer," he says. "Do you have somewhere to be?"

She glances at her closed laptop, the untouched emails waiting like obedient soldiers. "No," she says. "But I am not sure the baristas signed up for midlife emotional autopsies."

He smiles. "We could walk."

***

They walk without choosing a direction, drifting along the cold Brooklyn streets as the air bites at their cheeks. Nadine is grateful. The sharpness keeps her present.

"So," Charles says, sliding his hands into his coat pockets. "I have been thinking about this since I saw you in that hallway."

"It's been four hours," she says. "That is a lot of thinking time."

"I am a go-getter," he replies.

"What did you think about?"

He looks at her for a moment, as if weighing something.

"I kept hearing your voice in my head," he says. "That last week. In London. You remember?"

She remembers.

He had just gotten the call from home that his father's condition had worsened. She had received confirmation that her visa paperwork had been processed. She was leaving at the end of the term, back to Trinidad and then to the States. They were standing at a freezing bus stop, their breath small clouds in the air.

"I remember you said it was too much to ask someone to wait," she says.

"I remember you agreed," he says. "Very quickly."

They turn down another street. A dog pulls its owner toward a patch of slush with grass poking out.

"Did you think about me?" she asks.

There it is. One of the questions that has circled her mind for two decades. She realizes it left a mark.

He slows, then stops on the sidewalk, facing her. His expression is open, vulnerable in a way she had not seen on many adult faces. Even less so, the adult faces of men.

"I thought about you more than was reasonable," he says. "More than was healthy. I thought about you when I could barely remember what day it was. I thought about you when I was driving my mother to chemo at six in the morning. I thought about you when I walked past the library, and there was some girl with her head bent over books and a scarf like yours, and I would feel my chest hurt."

Her eyes sting. She blinks hard.

"Your mum battled cancer?"

"Yes, valiantly. She's in remission. Eleven years now."

They stop outside the cutest bookshop window and scan the offerings on display.

He asks carefully, "Did you think about me?"

"Yes," she says. The word comes out rough. "Every time I heard someone laugh like you. Every time I heard a song you played for me. In airports, always. I would watch people, secretly hoping you would appear, which was absurd. We did not even live on the same continent, as far as I knew."

"Love does not respect geography," he says.

He said love like it is like a thing that happens to you, not a choice.

Her throat feels dry, irritated. She swallows. "Were we a near thing," she asks, "or a thing you ran from?"

He exhales, breath visible in the cold. "Both," he says. "We were a near thing because we met right when both our lives were exploding. And I ran. I am not going to lie to you. I did not fight for us."

"Why?" she asks.

"I didn't think I deserved you," he says.

The answer lands with devastating simplicity.

He looks away, then back. "Back then, I had no money. No stability. My father was sick, my siblings needed me, and my passport was a barrier in every room I entered. You were brilliant and fearless and walking into this wide mysterious future. I felt like a weight that would drag you under."

"You were never a burden," she says quickly.

"I know that now," he says. "Then, all I could see was that choosing me meant choosing chaos. So, I told myself I was being noble by not asking you to stay. The truth is, I was afraid. Afraid you would say no. Afraid you would say yes, and I would ruin your life. Afraid that if I asked you to wait and it did not work out, I would be the villain in your story."

They start walking again, slower.

"And you," he says almost inaudibly. "Did you run?"

She thinks about that girl she was, eyes permanently tired, jaw clenched, carrying expectations like stones in her bag. She had no practice at asking for anything that might be refused.

"I pretended not to care," she says. "Because I didn't know how to ask anyone to choose me."

He is watching her now, gaze fixed, no interruption, no protest.

"I came from a family where you don't ask," she says. "You take what is given and say thanks. You do not rock the boat. You don't make demands. So, when you said it was too much to ask me to wait, I agreed, because the alternative would have been to say, actually, I want you to ask. I want you to want me enough to be unreasonable."

Her voice shakes, then calms.

"I didn't know how to say that," she finishes. "So, I pretended it was casual. I told myself it was a fling. I packed my bags and smiled and told my friends it was all very mature."

"And then?" he prompts.

"And then I cried in the airplane bathroom over the North Atlantic like a banshee," she says briskly.

He closes his eyes briefly, as if pained by the image.

"I wish I had known," he says.

"I wish I had told you," she says.

They reach a small park, mostly empty. The trees are bare. The benches are cold metal, but they sit anyway.

For a while, they say nothing. The city carries on its intense pace around them. Charles looks at her, trying to read her expression. Her eyes follow a kid in a bright red jacket as he zooms past on a scooter, unbothered by the chill.

"Did you choose your life," Nadine asks at last, "or did your life choose you?"

He considers this.

"I think my life chose me first," he says. "Circumstances did. Family did. Immigration rules did. Then, little by little, I started choosing back. I said yes to a job that scared me. I moved to a country where I knew almost no one. I started therapy when I realized I was living entirely for other people. That was only eight years ago, by the way."

He pauses, smiles wryly, and says, "Slow learner."

"You?" he asks.

"It feels like my life was handed to me as a script," she says. "Be the good daughter. Get the degree. Make the safe choices. Do not embarrass anyone. For a long time, I followed it. Even my rebellion was respectable. Working too much at a nonprofit is not exactly wild. It is just a different flavor of sacrifice."

She rubs her gloved hands together.

"I realized recently that I have built a life that is solid and kind of beautiful," she says. "I like my work. I like my home. I like who I am, most days. But there is this pocket in my chest that stays empty. I filled it with busyness for a long time. Lately, it has been harder to ignore."

"Romance," he says.

"Intimacy," she says. "Romance is the frame. Intimacy is the picture."

He smiles. "Still a poet."

"Still a flatterer," she replies.

"So here we are," he says. "Middle-aged. Competent. Tired. Still carrying versions of the kids we were. And suddenly we are face to face with the ghost of our road not taken."

"Is that what we are?" she asks, sounding vulnerable. "A ghost?"

He doesn't answer right away, then he steers them somewhere deeper.

"I need to know something first," he says. "Would we have worked then? If we had tried?"

Her first impulse is to say yes, of course, that love conquers all, that they would have held hands across oceans. But she is old enough to know better.

"I think we would have destroyed each other," she says.

He nods, not surprised. "Me too."

"I was too insecure," she says. "Too desperate to prove myself. I would have resented every sacrifice I made and then hated myself for resenting you. I would have tried to be perfect for you until I broke."

"I would have made you my reason for everything," he says. "Which sounds romantic, but it isn't. It is pressure. I would have used you as an excuse to ignore my own healing. I would have tried to save you from things you didn't ask to be saved from. And I would have expected you to save me back."

She exhales. The honesty hurts, but it also feels like massaging a knotted muscle.

"So, then what is left?" she asks. "Just a beautiful story we almost had?"

He is silent for a long moment. Nadine thinks, *Hmmm, he is certainly more thoughtful than I remember.*

"Let me ask a different question," he says. "Is the love still alive, or is it just nostalgia?"

She thinks of seeing him in the hallway. How her body recognized him before her mind did. How his voice made something deep inside her sit up.

"I'm not having butterflies," she says. "I am not swept away. I'm standing here in my forties with my feet firmly on the ground."

"And?" he asks.

"And I care," she says simply. "I care about who you became. I am attracted to the man you are, not just the boy you were. When you talk, I want to listen. When you laugh, it feels like my lungs remember how to expand."

He exhales, like he's about to say what needs to be said, finally. "I feel the same," he says. "It is not fireworks. It is . . . recognition. Like hearing a song I loved and realizing it still hits, but in different places now."

She leans back slightly, eyes closed, breathing in the cold air. He looks down for a moment, thumb running along the seam of his glove. For a beat, neither of them speaks.

"What would you have done differently back then," she asks, voice barely above a breath, "if you had believed you deserved me?"

It's his turn to look up at the gray sky. Then, he looks back at her. "I would have told you I loved you," he says. "Plainly. Not hinting, not making jokes. I would have said, Nadine, I am in love with you. I am scared. My life is a mess. I do not know how we make this work, but I want to try. I would have risked embarrassing myself."

The words land in her like a late arrival finally home.

"I would have asked you to ask," she says. "I would have said, Charles, I don't want to be reasonable. I want you to be a little selfish and say, please stay, or please wait, or please believe that we are worth the trouble."

He looks stricken for a moment, as if seeing alternate versions of themselves moving through a different city, a different decade.

"Instead," he says, "we walked away."

"Instead," she echoes.

He shifts closer on the bench. Their knees almost touch. He angles his body toward her without realizing it, like his attention moves before he does. She finds it ridiculously endearing.

"I am not asking for forgiveness," he says. "I do not think forgiveness is the point. We were who we were. We weren't equipped for more."

"I agree," she says. "I do not need you to be sorry. I needed to know you cared. That I was not the only one holding a secret grief for something that never quite existed."

"You were not alone," he says. "Not for a second."

"Let me try to say this right," he says. "It's long overdue. I loved you. I loved you in that library, at that bus stop, on that night we stayed up talking about nothing and everything. I loved you, and Nadine, I carried that love quietly like contraband through my thirties. I compared every would-be lover to you. I carried my love for and memory of us with me . . . through every city, every move, every hard season . . . And the truth is, I never found anything that fit the space you left."

Her vision blurs. She lets the tears rise this time. They spill over warm on her cold cheeks.

"I have feelings for you, too," she says. "In a way that surprised the hell out of me today."

He reaches over, slow enough that she can pull back if she wants, and brushes his thumb gently under her eye, wiping away one tear. His hand is warm.

"So, what do we do with that?" she asks.

"Honestly," he says, "I don't know. We could call this closure. A beautiful reunion. Hug, exchange social media, watch each other's lives from a safe distance."

A slight ache builds beneath her ribs, and she rests her hand there for a moment, surprised by the intensity of it. It's her turn to be quiet.

"Or," he continues, "we could be stupid again, but in a different way. Stupid with intention. Try to see who we are now when we do not have oceans and visas and graduate exams in the way. Let something unfold at the speed of our current lives, not our memories or fears."

"That sounds like trying again," she says.

"It is not the same try," he replies. "Back then, I wanted you to fix the ache in me. Now I know that is my work. I am not asking you to save me. I am asking whether you want to get to know me as the man I have become. No fantasy. No guarantees."

The wind picks up. A loose plastic bag rolls past like a tumbleweed.

"I am not walking away this time," he says in a measured tone. "Not by default. Not because I am scared. If we decide not to do this, I want it to be because we actually looked at it and chose no, not because we flinched."

Something in his certainty tugs loose an old memory.

She studies his face. The lines at the corners of his eyes. The small scar near his eyebrow, she remembers, from when he walked into a low-hanging branch while walking too fast and reading *The Autobiography of Malcolm X*. She had pressed her thumb there afterward, half scolding, half laughing. At the same time, he insisted he was successfully "multitasking," and she told him being lost in a book didn't excuse him from nearly concussing himself. It had been early between them, but that moment, her fussing, his grinning, was the first time she realized she cared more than she meant to.

Nadine looks away, straightens her back, and crosses one leg over the other, angling away from him.

She thinks about her tidy apartment. Her carefully arranged life, balanced on the assumption that anything big and messy will hurt her.

She also thinks about how alive she felt in that courthouse hallway the moment she heard his voice.

She turns to him and asks, "What would trying look like?"

He smiles, eyes twinkling. "It would look like coffee again. Dinner. Telling the awkward stories of the last twenty years, not just the polished versions. Meeting each other's messy friends. Letting my mother interrogate you on WhatsApp. Letting your cousins size me up at Sunday lunch. It would look like patience. We are not in our twenties anymore; we cannot upheave our lives overnight. But we can be here for each other. Consistently. We can be honest when we are triggered by old fears."

"You make it sound very unromantic," she says, though there is a warmth spreading in her chest.

"I have lost the taste for romance that ignores reality," he says. "Through therapy, I have a new appreciation for the kind that holds reality and leans way in."

She considers her own fear. It is there, coiled in her stomach. Fear of disappointment. Fear of losing the clean edges of the life she built.

But there is also curiosity about what can be. The feeling is sharp and hopeful.

"I do not know," she says slowly, "if I have any middle-aged romantic bandwidth left."

He laughs. "I appreciate your honesty."

"But," she adds, feeling the word open something, "I know this. When I walked away from you at that bus stop, I felt like I was leaving a page unfinished. I do not want to repeat that. I do not want to look back in ten years and think, oh, I met him again, and I chose my emails instead of . . . this."

"So?" he asks.

She turns her hand over on the bench, palm up, an invitation.

"So I am not walking away this time either," she says. "Let's not name it yet. We see if what we feel now is strong enough to live in the same space as our past."

His expression relaxes, and he lets his spine rest into the slats, no longer sitting so upright. Relief and gratitude move across his face, edged with a hint of wonder. He takes her hand. His palm is warm, his grip gentle but sure.

"Okay," he says. "Then let us start small. Tonight. Dinner. There is a Senegalese place in Bed-Stuy, your neighborhood, I have been wanting to try. You will let me argue with you about jollof, and you will tell me why Caribbean seasoning is superior."

She snorts. "I do not need dinner for that argument. I can win it right here."

"Confidence," he says, smiling. "I like it."

He stands and keeps her hand in his, tugging lightly. "Come on. Let us walk you home. We can argue on the way."

She hesitates. "It is a bit far."

"We have twenty years to catch up on," he says. "A long walk seems appropriate."

She looks at their joined hands. Feels the slight tremor in her own. Also feels the solid ground under her feet.

"Okay," she says.

They walk. Their arms brush now and then, the contact small but thrilling. They talk about music first. It's safer ground. They compare playlists. Then they talk about the scariest medical tests their parents have had. The petty reasons they ended past relationships. The book reads that got them through lonely winters.

It is not a movie montage. There are awkward pauses and moments where one of them says, "Let's save that story for another day; I am not ready to open that box."

But there is also laughter. Stop-the-walk-hold-their-belly laughter. The kind that feels like oxygen.

As they cross a busy avenue, the light changes, and they have to hurry. Nadine instinctively reaches for his arm. *Oh, yes, I remember this,* she thinks.

At her building, they stop.

"This is me," she says.

He looks up at the brownstone, then back at her.

"Can I see you again on purpose?" he asks. "Not by the justice system's design."

She smiles. "You have my number. If you do not text, you will be haunted by my disappointed Caribbean auntie energy forever."

He winces theatrically. "Terrifying. I will text."

They stand there for a minute, neither quite ready to break the moment.

"Thank you," she says. "For being honest. For not pretending this is just funny or casual."

"Thank you," he replies. "For not pretending it did not matter."

He leans in slowly, giving her time to step back. She does not. Their lips meet in the softest of kisses, barely more than a press. It is not about heat. It is an acknowledgment, a punctuation mark at the end of a long, unsent sentence.

When they separate, they both exhale a little laugh, shy and surprised.

"Okay," he says. "Now I am definitely texting."

She laughs. "Good."

Inside, as she climbs the stairs to her apartment, her heart does not race the wild way it did when she was twenty-two. She is calm. Awake.

She knows there is no guarantee. They could date for a few months and realize they are better as friends. Old patterns could surface, requiring work neither of them is willing to do. Life could throw more curveballs. Parents get sick. Jobs disappear. People change.

But for the first time in a long time, she feels herself choosing, not just being carried along.

Her phone buzzes as she slips off her shoes.

"Made it halfway down the block and already missed you. Is that too corny?"

She smiles and types, "Yes, but I appreciate the honesty."

She sets the phone down, leans against her front door, and lets herself feel the strange, calm joy of having met him again and bravely telling the truth. Of hearing it back.

Whatever happens next is not a fantasy of the life they did not live. It is this life, with its wrinkles and responsibilities and grown-up schedules.

It is a chance, not to redo their twenties, but to meet each other where they are now.

And this time, they both know how to say out loud, that they want to be chosen.

24

Code Black, Code White

— ♥ —

I should've been at the hospital twenty minutes ago. I didn't know it yet, but my internal clock wasn't the only thing that had been reset that morning. The snow drifted down lazily; the city muffled under a hush that made even New York seem contemplative.

I'd been running on autopilot ever since I moved from the West Coast three months ago. Every day before work, I stopped at the coffee shop two blocks from the hospital and picked up the largest cup of black coffee to go. The homeless man swung the door open every day, straightened up, and said, "Hey, doc." I would give him a quick chin-up as I passed, and he would catch it with a nod of his own.

Today seemed like the same old. The place was swollen with the low drone of multiple conversations and the hiss of milk steaming somewhere behind the counter. As I stood in line, I touched my chin, realizing too late that I'd missed a spot while shaving that morning. Betina, the Puerto Rican barista, flashed her usual smile when she saw me. She'd already scrawled, "Harry" on a large cup before I even ordered.

"Got your usual ready, handsome," she said, sliding the lid on with a wink.

"Thanks, Betina." Not one for flirting with women, I offered her a polite half-smile that didn't quite reach my eyes and turned away.

Running late, I should have left right then. Yet, something about the morning and this place gave me pause. The air was warm against the November chill outside, the scent of roasted beans, nutmeg, and cinnamon heavy in the room. I glanced around, spotted the only open seat, and sat.

The woman beside me didn't seem to notice I was there. She watched the street, fingers circling the rim of her mug, lost in thought. She was wearing navy scrubs. *Hospital attire*, I guessed. A doctor, maybe. I tried to focus on the emails on my phone, but my attention kept drifting back to her. There was something about the way she sat. She seemed composed yet cautious, as if she were holding the pieces of herself together. I was curious.

The loud ticking of the clock behind us was the only other thing that arrested my attention.

"That clock ticking is loud, isn't it?" The words directed toward her escaped before I could stop them.

She turned. I was not prepared for that face. She had smooth, dark skin, a Nefertiti-shaped face, red lips, and light brown eyes, showing surprise. I must have looked like a deer in the headlights staring at her. She studied me for a beat that felt like an eternity.

"Um . . ." she uttered.

"I've rendered you speechless?" I tried for charm and probably landed on awkward.

She didn't answer. I filled the silence. "Okay, never mind." I looked out the window, pretending peace while my pulse sprinted.

Her gaze brushed me again. I could feel her eyes on me, assessing, not shy. "I like your coat," she said finally, voice like honey and aged whiskey.

I glanced down at the black wool coat my father had given me when I started my residency. "Thanks. It was a gift."

"From someone who loves you," she said, not asking.

"My dad. He has a dozen like it. Says a good coat commands respect."

"Your father sounds wise."

"He is. He and my mom adopted me when I was two. He's Black, Mom's Chinese American." I hesitated. *Why did I offer this information? But I did not, could not, stop.* "They took in lots of foster kids. I was the only one they adopted."

She raised her neatly threaded eyebrows.

"Harrison Chen-Williams," I said, extending my hand. "Most people call me Harry."

She hesitated for a few long seconds before responding.

"Dr. Amara Brooks." Her hand was warm, grip firm. And it fit in mine.

I didn't let go right away. Her palm felt like déjà vu, like we'd done this in another lifetime. I felt something change in me then. I wasn't sure what, but I knew I'd be a fool not to see where this went.

She looked away. "You remind me of . . ." she started and then seemed to realize she was speaking out loud and cut herself off. She shook her head and said, "Sorry. It's been a morning."

My phone buzzed. It was the fellowship coordinator. "I'm late for rounds."

"You're a doctor too? Which hospital?"

"Presbyterian. Cardiothoracic fellowship."

Her mouth dropped. "You're the new fellow? Harry from Stanford?"

"Guilty. You know the program?"

"I'm a second-year internal medicine resident there. I am amazed we never saw each other at the hospital." She shook her head, smiling. "Dr. Peterson's been talking about you nonstop. The golden boy who turned down Hopkins."

"Wait, I think I heard of you, too. Are you the Dr. Brooks who caught that endocarditis case everyone missed?"

Her eyes widened. "You heard about that?"

"Are you kidding? Orientation wouldn't shut up about it. I thought you were . . ."

"A man?" She chuckled.

Silence dropped between us, and I could kick myself for what I said. I had to do something. I stood, gathering nerve.

"Walk with me? Since we're going to the same place?"

She didn't answer immediately. Her gaze drifted toward the window as she finished the last of her drink, with deliberate gulps. I looked at her neck again, then at her hands around the mug. The tendons in her wrist flexed, and a small pulse fluttered just below her ear. I watched and waited, like a man forgetting his place. *What is going on, Harry? You don't do this.*

When she finally rose, sliding the chair back with a quiet scrape, something in me calmed and unraveled all at once.

We walked. She talked about medicine the way poets talk about rain, half wonder, half devotion. I wondered if she had someone special. I hoped there wasn't.

At the hospital doors, before we parted ways, I risked it. "Drinks tonight?"

"I don't really . . ." She paused, reconsidered. "You know what? Sure. But the sober bar. I don't drink much."

"The mocktail bar it is."

***

Three weeks later, the mocktail bar knew our orders by heart. Amara, elderflower-ginger fizz. Me, anything citrus.

We began to seek each other out at the hospital, too. Or maybe that was me, choosing to take breaks on her floor.

"You're different," she said one evening in the on-call room, both of us nursing cold coffee.

"Different how?"

"I have a type. Had a type." She stared at her cup. "Black men. Hispanic men. Usually emotionally unavailable. Something casual, flameout quick. But you, you're available. To be honest, that terrifies me."

I did not know what to say. Or rather, I was afraid of saying the wrong thing. I knew this moment was important. So, I remained quiet, waiting for her to finish.

"I usually rush in, sleep with someone by the third date, and crash by month three. With you . . . I want it to be different. I don't want to rush."

"I can wait."

She looked at me then. "Why?" she asked, studying me in that unblinking way doctors do. "You could have anyone."

Before I could respond, she tilted her head. "Tall, lanky, the good kind of serious. You've got that clean-cut thing. Like a young Leonardo DiCaprio in *Catch Me If You Can*. A man, a doctor, who actually listens."

She shrugged and continued. "Professional, obviously affluent, maybe a little too WASPy for your own good."

I laughed despite myself. "That's . . . oddly specific."

"Occupational hazard," she said. "We notice details."

I paused, feeling put on the spot with her question, description of me, and statement. I held her gaze and then made a decision. Unlike my other relationships, I would open up, the part I never offered anyone else, born from being the kid who learned not to need too much because foster families change fast when you're the one being moved around. *I will let Amara know that I see her and I want her.*

"Because you quote Toni Morrison during rounds. Because you sneak extra pudding to Mr. Hendrickson in 302. Because when you think no one's looking, you do a victory dance after a good procedure. Because you sing when you're stressed, and I love your voice."

I finished listing the particular things I saw in her, the things I loved. The small lamp on the table threw a warm pool of light between us. She stared at me as if she had not expected to be seen that clearly.

"You are extraordinary, Amara. You do not even want to acknowledge it."

She pulled back a little, blinking fast. Her fingers squeezed the cup, and she looked down, I supposed, to calm herself.

I reached across the table and let my fingertips brush hers. Not a grab. Not a claim. Just a point of connection. She froze, then slowly turned her hand so our fingers slipped together. The contact startled both of us. She breathed in sharply, soft and unguarded.

For a moment, we stayed like that, hands tangled, the air warm and charged.

She leaned in without seeming to know she was doing it, drawn by something quiet and certain. Her lips hovered close to mine. I felt her breath on my mouth.

"You are taking us slow, remember," I whispered.

Still, I did not pull away. I let the tip of my nose graze the corner of her mouth, slow enough to register, not enough to cross the line. Her pulse jumped under her skin, and she closed her eyes for a long second.

Her phone lit up on the table and vibrated.

Malik: *Where are you?*

The magic of the moment broke. She exhaled hard and slipped her hand from mine, pulling back just enough to gather herself.

"I have to go."

Her voice was calm, but she did not look at me right away. When she finally did, her eyes were warmer. Softer.

She blinked again, entirely breaking the spell. "I have to go," she said again. "My brother's waiting."

It was the first time she had mentioned family in the present tense.

***

"You're distracted," Mom said on FaceTime. Behind her, Dad was making dumplings in their Berkeley kitchen.

"I'm not distracted," I said.

"You're smiling at your phone."

Dad called from somewhere in the room and said, "He met someone, Angie?"

"I think so," Mom said. "What's her name?"

"Amara. She's a resident."

Dad popped into frame, flour in his beard. "Amara? Nice name.

She Black?"

"Marcus!"

"What? I'm asking. Maybe she can teach this boy about seasoning he never learned from us."

Mom rolled her eyes. "We're coming to New York next month for your father's conference. We'll stay with you."

My stomach dropped. "When?"

"January fifteenth. And we expect to meet this Amara."

After they hung up, I texted her.

Me: *Hypothetical question*

Amara: *Those are never hypothetical*

Me: *If someone's parents were coming to town, and that someone needed a favor, would you consider helping?*

Amara: *Depends on the favor*

Me: *Pretend to be my girlfriend so they don't set me up with their colleague's daughter?*

Amara: *You want me to meet your parents as your fake girlfriend?*

Me: *I know*

It's crazy

The chat went still, no typing dots. My lungs seemed to forget their job. Then her bubble flickered back to life, and I exhaled like a man reprieved.

Amara: *I'll do it. But I have conditions*

Me: *Hit me*

Amara: *1 No lying to your parents. If they ask, this isn't serious yet we're just seeing where it goes*

2 PG-13 in public. Hand-holding allowed. Kissing: sparingly

3 We debrief after every meeting. No letting awkward stuff fester

4 Stop the bit the minute either of us wants the real thing or none

How long will they be in town?

Me: *A week in January. Let's add an addendum: safe word if things get chaotic.*

Amara: . . .

Pineapple

Me: *acknowledged. I'll be a phenomenal fake boyfriend.*

Amara: *Prove it, Chen-Williams.*

***

On December 20th, I was packing for a flight home when she called with her own proposal.

"I've been thinking about your fake girlfriend proposal," she said.

"And?"

"My family's having a Christmas party tomorrow. My mother specifically. If I'm meeting yours, I suppose you should meet mine."

She exhaled and continued. "Fair warning, it'll be a very Black affair. Aunties with opinions. Uncles making jokes about white people's potato salad."

"I make excellent potato salad."

"With raisins?"

"God, no."

She laughed. "Harry, I'm serious. Mom's going to have a lot to say about this. My brother Malik is protective. My ex might be there."

Her voice dropped when she said my name. *Harry.*

I was replaying my name in her way, feeling the sound of it settle low in my chest, before my eyebrows knotted as my brain tripped over something else she said.

"Your ex?"

"Darius. Corner-store owner near Mom's place. It was right after my dad died." She sighed. "Bad timing, poor decisions. I'm okay if you don't want to do this?"

Meet her family and her ex? The neurons in my brain staged a small electrical protest, sparks flying in all directions.

"Never mind, it's . . ."

"I want to," I said, faster than I meant to.

"Are you sure?"

"I'm sure."

***

The brownstone in Bed-Stuy pulsed with music and perfume, the bass line shaking through the floorboards like a second heartbeat. Coats hung from the banister, and the smell of baked ham and nutmeg drifted from the kitchen. I stood near the entryway, the only white man in the room; everyone knew it, and I felt myself sticking out like a missing brushstroke in a familiar painting.

"So, you're the white boy," her mother, Denise, said by way of hello. She was Amara in twenty years, same high cheekbones, same don't-waste-my-time look in her light brown eyes.

"Mom."

"What? I'm saying what they're thinking." Denise eyed me while speaking to Amara. Then, turning back to her, she added, "I was not expecting him to actually come. He's brave."

"Because I'm white?" I asked, managing half a smile.

"Because Amara's never brought anyone home."

From somewhere behind us, a man's voice cut through the crowd. "Come on, man, before Mom starts interrogating you."

He clapped a hand on my shoulder and guided me through the hallway to a smaller room where the men had gathered. The air was dense with cologne and laughter, a domino game clacking at one end of the table, someone debating whether the Knicks would ever find redemption.

"I'm Malik," he said, handing me a drink, already grinning.

Relax, Harry, relax, I told myself.

The room was alive with overlapping jokes and arguments, someone betting the Knicks would ruin Christmas again. Yet somehow the quieter voices from the next room wafted through it all, finding me.

Girl lost her mind.

What would her daddy think?

Least he's a doctor.

The words drifted in like smoke, faint but impossible to ignore. I took a sip, leaned toward Malik, and said something about the Knicks' chances this decade to prove I was still listening. When someone cracked a joke that sent the room into laughter, I used the noise to slip out.

I wanted to find Amara.

In the kitchen, her Auntie Jo thrust a pan at me. "You helping, white boy, or just pretty?"

"I can help," I said, eagerly slipping on nearby mitts that proved to be too small. Amara bumped my hip as she reached for the mac and cheese.

"You take the left; I'll take the right."

I felt my whole demeanor relax. Our shoulders touched. A faint smear of cranberry sauce glimmered on the lobe of her ear; I wiped it away with my thumb and sucked before thinking. She held still, as if she was afraid to breathe.

"Mind the rating of this scene, Harry," she whispered.

"Copy."

Then Darius arrived, dark-skinned like everyone else here, gregarious, familiar. He hugged Amara for a moment too long.

"So, you're the rebound," he said to me, not unkindly, but with a warning tucked somewhere beneath the words.

"Depends on who's asking."

"Question is, do you know who you are in this space?"

I held his gaze. "I do. I'm the man she brought home."

The kitchen erupted in stifled whoops and laughter. A spoon hit the side of a pot, and someone whispered an impressed, "Alright now." I tried to act unfazed, but my pulse was buzzing.

Then I saw her.

Amara had backed away from us, toward the doorway, and was looking at me. Nothing was said, but the whole room seemed to pull away from us. The music, jokes, and crowd faded away. I saw only her. Her lips parted in a small, stunned smile. She looked as if she were in heat, and my whole being responded.

Yes, I'm your man, I thought.

At the worst moment ever, someone bumped my shoulder on their way to the fridge. The spell broke as I wobbled. I blinked hard and stepped back toward the counter.

Before I could say or do anything else, another aunt tugged Amara toward the living room where the music was loudest. From my spot at the counter, I watched her slip easily into the crowd. Her hips caught the rhythm, laughter bubbling up as relatives drew her in. The light from the chandelier hit her skin like gold.

Confidence is easy in a duel, harder in a room full of people who already claim her. She laughed, she moved, she belonged. I moved to the doorway, wondering if love alone could ever make me with her feel like home, too.

The warmth of the kitchen pressed against me. I turned and slipped out the back door.

Outside, Malik was already on the porch overlooking the garden dusted with snow, a cigar burning low between his fingers. "It's a lot?" he asked, offering a beer.

"It's fine."

"No, it's not. Look, I like you. But you need to get this . . . Amara's never done the interracial thing. Bringing you home? Huge. After Daddy died, she dated men she couldn't get too close to."

"And I'm different?"

"You tell me."

"My dad's Black," I said quietly.

Malik blinked. "What?"

"I'm adopted. Dad is Black. Mom's Chinese."

"Well, damn, she did not tell me that." He laughed, leaning back until the old metal chair sighed beneath him.

I'd seen their father in a framed photo on the bookshelf in Amara's apartment. In it, he was smiling broadly, cigarette poised between fingers, dark skin gleaming under a New York City sun. Malik had the same warmth about him, though softened with age and comfort. His face was fuller, his eyes kinder, his body carried the easy weight of someone who never missed a good meal. He hooked an ankle over his knee, beer dangling from his fingers.

"Still doesn't make it easy. You move through the world white."

"I know. But I also know what it means to love across difference. I watched my parents do it my whole life."

He studied me. "You love her?"

"I'm getting there."

Malik didn't answer. We fell into a comfortable silence. He leaned back in his chair, one ankle resting over his knee, the glow from his cigar ember pulsing. Inside, someone laughed too loudly, and the sound tumbled out onto the enclosed porch before settling back into quiet.

Amara appeared in the doorway. "Everything okay?"

Malik took one last draw on his cigar, the tip flaring bright, then tapped the ash neatly into a nearby planter. "Your boy's alright," he said, standing and brushing off his hands. He gave me a knowing look. "Don't screw it up, Harrison."

He disappeared inside, with the scent of tobacco and laughter trailing after him.

"I'm ready to go, Harry."

"Okay." I stood and pulled her to me, conscious of the part I was trying on.

We glided together from cluster to cluster, stopping to say goodbye to every aunt, cousin, and family friend who mattered. It took longer than I expected.

The Uber pulled away from the curb, and a quiet settled in fast. Amara sat close enough that our coats brushed each time the car shifted lanes. Her thigh rested near mine, not touching, but close enough that I could feel the warmth radiating through the fabric. The city lights flared across her face in soft flashes, and I let myself look, remembering her energy from earlier.

She kept her gaze on the window, hands clasped in her lap, but I saw the tension in her shoulders. I was sure she felt the closeness, too.

"I'm sorry," she said finally. "I shouldn't have brought you there."

"Why?"

"Because now you know how complicated this would be."

"Amara, I'm not playing games. I know exactly how complicated it is. My parents have been proving love across lines for thirty years."

"It's different."

"You're right. They stuck together when things got tough. My dad taught me, love isn't finding someone who fits your world, it's building a new one together."

Tears welled up in her eyes. "I don't know how to do this without armor."

"Then keep it on until you feel safe."

"What if I never do?"

"Then I'll love you in your armor."

She didn't answer, just looked at me, calm and open. The car hit a pothole; we swayed closer, and my arms wrapped around her shoulder and pulled her in.

When we kissed, it wasn't fireworks; it was a fuse catching: quiet, inevitable, hungry. A fitting end to the evening and the moment I knew the pretending was over on my side, though I had no idea if she was crossing that line with me.

***

Christmas in Berkeley was torture. I called Amara every morning, texted all day, and FaceTimed at night. My parents noticed.

"Just fly her out," Dad said the day after Christmas.

"It's still Christmas. She's with her family."

"And you're miserable." He joined me on the porch.

Inside, the house was alive with sound. My father's sisters and my mother were in the kitchen comparing spice blends, arguing softly about whether cloves belonged in black cake. The television in the den carried the Warriors game, the announcer's voice rising over the pop of the fireplace. I could smell fake pine and nutmeg scents from the tree we'd kept since I was a kid.

"What's really going on?" Dad asked.

I told him about the party, about feeling like an intruder.

"Good," he said.

"Good?"

"You should feel it. That's the tax of difference." His voice came out strong and certain, the kind that carried through walls.

Mom stepped onto the porch with two mugs of cocoa, her shawl bright against the soft gray morning. "Marcus, use your inside voice. Harrison, come help with the lights after you and your father finish solving racism. Your aunts are driving me crazy."

Dad grinned, unbothered. I took the cocoa from her, grateful for the warmth and the interruption.

We laughed, but later that night, Dad continued.

"She's strong," he said, scrolling on his tablet. "Impressive résumé. And she's lived a little, posts regularly, has friends, an ex or two. You're not on her feed a lot, just one post of the two of you at a holiday event. Looks like a house party."

"Dad, did you just Google, LinkedIn, and IG my girlfriend?"

"Basic vetting," he said.

Mom looked up from her knitting. "Marcus."

He lifted a palm. "I'm just saying she's got velocity. You fall slowly and deeply. She moves fast. Don't mistake survival for sin."

It took me a second to realize we weren't just talking about life in general. We were talking about Amara, about the men who came before me, about the trail of names I'd pretended not to notice when she spoke of her past.

Mom set her yarn aside, came over, and touched my shoulder. "Grief scrambles people. She lost her father young. Sometimes the body heals before the heart catches up."

I nodded. "She told me that herself. She said she wants to do this differently with me."

"Then meet her there," Mom said. "Not where you think she should be. And don't ever make her feel she has to earn a clean slate."

Dad sighed. "I know I referenced it, but she's not a résumé, son. Just love who she's becoming."

Mom smiled. "Go call her, Harrison. Let her know she's safe with you."

***

On New Year's Eve, we were three thousand miles apart. She was at a party in Harlem, the kind that overflowed with laughter, glassware, and music that pulsed through the phone when she answered my call just before midnight.

"Almost the countdown," she said, breathless. I could hear people cheering behind her, someone shouting for more champagne.

"Wish you were here."

"Wish I was too."

Through the receiver, I pictured her in a shimmer of gold, surrounded by people who belonged to her world. The space between us felt sharper than the distance. A man's voice, Caribbean accent, came through faintly, asking if she was ready for the toast. She laughed, said something I couldn't make out.

"You good?" I asked.

"Yeah," she said quickly, but the noise swallowed the rest of her answer.

Fireworks cracked outside my parents' house. I watched them from the porch, each burst lighting the quiet street in color before dying into smoke. When I looked back at my phone, the call had ended.

I flew to New York the next afternoon. The city felt colder than I remembered. Her texts came slower. Neither of us said what had changed, but somewhere between the countdown and the landing, I knew we were no longer pretending. I just wasn't sure what we were now.

***

We both had duty schedules we couldn't escape, so when we finally stole an afternoon on the eighth day of the new year, we walked Central Park like tourists and let our hands brush without deciding what it meant.

As we reached the fountain, she paused, watching the ice gather along the edges. "Your parents still coming?"

"Next weekend."

She glanced at me, a small smile tugging at her lips. "So . . . we're still pretending?"

"Only if you're still willing."

"I'll play along," she said, slipping her hand into mine. "But at some point, you'll have to tell me when the act ends."

I wanted to ask about New Year's, about the voice I'd heard on the phone and the laugh that didn't sound like mine. Instead, I said, "You have a good time at the ball drop party?"

She looked over, surprised. "It was loud. You didn't miss much."

I nodded, pretending that was enough.

***

January fifteenth crept up like a test I'd studied for and still didn't feel ready to take. We'd agreed to the bit, pretending to date for my parents' sake, but neither of us seemed capable of treating it as a joke. Whatever this was, it had stopped feeling fake a long time ago.

Amara sat on my couch in a tiny black dress that short-circuited my common sense and erased my vocabulary. I walked the length of my living room, which wasn't long to begin with, then turned, crossed it again, and circled back to the kitchen. The charcuterie board looked fine. It also looked like a cry for help.

"Stop pacing," she said. "You're making me nervous."

"They're going to know."

"They already suspect, I'm sure," she said with a small smile. "But we agreed to the story, remember?"

Right . . . *the story*. The one where we were only pretending to be in a relationship. I wasn't sure she still believed that, or if she just needed to. Maybe I did too.

"Then we'd better make it convincing." She stood and crossed to me, close enough for the scent of her perfume to stir every nerve I was trying to calm. She tugged my collar straight, slowly and with sensual force. Her fingers were calm. Mine, by my side, weren't.

"Rehearsal," she murmured. "If this is going to work, we should look easy together."

I nodded, calibrating my sense of self, pretending I understood which part of this was still imitation.

"Us?" I slid my hands up to the small of her back and drew her to me. "We're graduate level easy."

She rose onto her toes and pressed a slow, assessing kiss to my mouth, then another, softer. Heat gathered with nowhere to be theatrical about it.

We broke apart slowly, neither of us rushing to end it. Her eyes stayed closed for one long beat, and when she opened them, she did not step back. I searched her face for a hint of regret and found none. She studied me with a quiet question in her eyes, as if waiting to see whether I would treat the kiss as an accident or a choice.

I lifted a hand to her jaw and stroked the line just beneath her ear. She leaned into my touch before she seemed aware of it. The space between us felt thinner than it had ever been.

"Mm."

"Grading?" I asked, dazed.

"B plus," she said, pupils wide. "Docked for showing your whole heart on the first try."

"I'm an overachiever," I whispered. "I can do extra credit."

Her laugh dissolved against my lips . . . and then the door burst open.

"Surprise! We caught an earlier flight . . . Oh!" Mom stopped, and Dad nearly collided with her shoulder. Keys clattered. Luggage thunked. New York wind barreled in with them.

Amara turned in my arms like she'd rehearsed that move her whole life. "You must be the parents I've heard so much about. I'm Amara."

Chaos followed. Chen-Williams' brand. Mom adopted her in under sixty seconds, ushering her in with a stream of questions about sleep, food, and rotations. Dad interrogated her specialty while also offering to make tea, rearrange my bookshelf, and fix my drafty window. By the time we made it onto the 7 train to Flushing, they'd asked a hundred questions and got answers for fewer than half, which is how my family says, "We like you."

"This place has a Michelin star?" Amara whispered, eyeing the modest storefront when we arrived.

"Mom doesn't believe in fancy," I whispered back. "She believes in authenticity."

The owner greeted my parents in Mandarin; Mom answered with happy fluency, and Dad chimed in with commentary in English. We sat at their usual table, where dishes we hadn't ordered arrived, along with a pot of a tea my mother believes heals everything.

"So," Mom said, serving Amara soup dumplings as if Amara had always sat there, "tell us how you really met. Not the coffee shop story. The actual story."

"It was a coffee shop," I insisted.

"But there's more," Dad said, studying Amara with affection. "Were you watching him, or was he watching you?"

"I was watching the street," Amara said softly. "Thinking about my father. He passed five years ago." She looked at me. "Harry interrupted my thoughts with a comment about a loud clock. I wasn't kind at first."

She smiled and continued. "But he wore this black coat. My father loved black wool coats. Seeing him for a moment felt like . . . permission. Like my daddy telling me to pay attention."

Dad put his hand over hers and smiled. "I got that coat for Harry. The elders and ancestors guide us to what we need."

"You believe that?" she asked.

"I believe love shows up in places that make no sense to anybody but the two people in it," he said. "Ask Angela. I was supposed to marry a nice Trinidadian girl that my mother picked out. Then I met your future mother-in-law at a protest."

Dad slipped those words in. *Did she not catch them? "Future mother-in-law."* My pulse tripped over the phrase. I kept my expression neutral, took another sip of tea, and let the conversation move on without me.

"Which one?" Amara asked, a grin sneaking out.

"Does it matter?" Mom said dryly. "It was the eighties."

"He posted my bail," Mom added.

"Romantic," I muttered.

"It was," Mom said.

Amara's smile warmed the table. We were doing it. And then Dad's curiosity, the part that serves him beautifully as a physician and less beautifully as a father, edged too close to the line.

"So, Amara," he began, zeroing his chopsticks at nothing in particular, "young people date differently these days. I imagine."

"Marcus," Mom said, his name in a tone of a warning bell.

He blinked, caught himself, and set the chopsticks down. "I imagine," he rephrased carefully, "that loving after loss looks different. I'm glad you told Harrison who you were when you met. That's all I wanted to say."

Relief flashed across Amara's face, quick, then gone. Under the table, she threaded her ankle around mine, casual to anyone watching but anchoring to me. I answered with a slight squeeze. We were still acting, but our bodies hadn't gotten the memo.

The conversation moved to lighter terrain. Residency schedules. Dumpling technique. The time Dad tried to bribe a cat to love him with sashimi. The owner brought out a dish Mom swears is medicine. We were laughing when Dad took a breath and aimed straight for the heart.

"When will you two start this for real?" he asked.

"Marcus!" Mom swatted him, only half pretending.

Amara looked at me, and something in her expression unclasped. "We're figuring it out," she said. "Aren't we?"

My heart jumped toward her. "Are we?"

"I'd like to," she said. "If you would."

"God, yes."

Dad cleared his throat. "We're still here," he reminded the two idiots admitting love across the scallion pancakes.

But I was already leaning across the table, kissing her like the first time I tasted oxygen. When I sat back, Mom was misty, Dad looked smug, and Amara glanced from my mouth to my eyes and back, as if memorizing, forever.

"Finally," Dad said. "Now, let's discuss something vital. Amara, can you cook? Because this boy burns water."

We all laughed. The rest of dinner spun golden. Amara relaxed into my side; my nervous system, usually tuned to disaster, learned a new frequency: OK.

On the walk back to the train station, Dad kept me a few steps behind the women, who were already arm-in-arm and plotting dumpling lessons.

"She's the one."

"How do you know?"

"Because she doesn't just look at you, she understands you. And because when I aimed my mouth at something unhelpful, your mother called me back to sense, but Amara didn't flinch. She's calm when it counts."

He paused. "I saw your face when I nearly asked about her past. You were ready to put your body between her and us if you had to. Good. Do that. But remember what we told you at Christmas: she isn't a résumé. Leave the old pages alone. Read who she is now."

"I hear you."

"When she's ready, I'd like to meet her mother," he added.

Back at my place, after my parents said goodnight, Amara and I sat, huddled together on the stoop.

"I need to tell you something," she said. "I'm falling for you. Not quick-burn falling. The other kind. Slow. Calm. I don't know how to do slow."

"We'll figure it out together." I hugged her closer.

"I'm not a project."

"You're a person preserving herself," I said. "I'm lucky I get a front-row seat."

She kissed me, even deeper than the rehearsal, sure in a way that made these promises feel like facts.

"Your dad's right," she whispered against my mouth. "He told me you are my one."

"Yeah? I appreciate his meddling for a change."

"Yeah. But if you tell him I said that, I'll deny it."

I laughed and then kissed her forehead. "Deal."

***

The week after my parents flew home, hospital life tried its best to grind us up. A code at dawn stole a night of sleep. A consult turned into a twelve-hour case. A group of residents discovered the world of mocktails and took over our table. We learned to live in the margins: stolen coffees, stairwell check-ins, calls from cabs. The fake-dating bit evaporated without ceremony. We didn't need it anymore.

One night, late, we ducked into the empty teaching kitchen off the residents' lounge. Someone had left a tray of brownies, which we pretended were dinner.

"Question," she said, licking chocolate from her thumb, then stopping when she realized I was watching. "PG-13," she reminded both of us with a half smile.

"Still? Nah, let's seek an R-rating." I was only half joking. She swatted my arm.

"Ask me anything," I said.

"What does your inner voice tell you about us when you're not performing optimism for me?" she asked.

"Performing?"

"You're always playing nice, Harry. Always finding the silver lining, like you're afraid if you don't smile, something will fall apart."

I sat back. "Maybe I am."

She watched me for a moment. "Darius was the same way at first. Always bright, always calm. Then I realized it was a shield. He needed me to need him, which I didn't. And the others . . . they were all me searching for my father's love in somebody else's arms. I ended each one feeling hollow. Now I understood that what I wanted wasn't in their touch, or their bodies, or their promises."

I let her words settle. She wasn't confessing; she was naming a wound that had finally stopped bleeding.

"I can't compete with the memory of your father's love, Amara."

She looked up, startled.

"I don't want to," I added. "I just want to be here. Whatever that looks like, however long it lasts."

She studied me, measuring what I'd said.

"And I'm not trying to fix you," I continued.

Her gaze softened. "Then what are you doing?"

"Trying to stay. Even when it's uncomfortable." I took a breath. "And for the record, I didn't love hearing another man's voice on New Year's Eve."

I watched her face and realized I had brought up something she wasn't carrying. Whatever the New Year's call had meant to me, it hadn't lived that long in her mind.

She nodded slowly. "You feel things deeply, Harry. I'm still learning how to do that." She hesitated, then said, "And I'm learning what it means to be in something with another person. To think about how what I do, what I don't even think about, lands on them, especially when that someone is you.

"Nothing happened, Harry. I was not with another man. I kissed no one when the ball dropped, but I did dance and had a lot of fun.

"Since we met, there has been no one with me physically or emotionally. You are my one and only."

The matter-of-fact honesty in her voice felt like an offering, small but real.

She reached for my hand, and stillness gathered between us, not empty but alive.

Somewhere down the hall, my pager buzzed. Hers followed a second later.

We looked at each other, the spell breaking.

"Code Black," she said, reading hers.

"Code White," I answered.

For a beat, neither of us moved. Then we both stood, professionals again, carrying whatever this was back into the world that always called us first.

We had small firsts and big ones: the first time Malik texted me a meme and then followed it with: she likes lilies, not roses, do with that what you will, which is how I learned about the flowers I now associate with every lucky Tuesday we both had off; the first time a stranger on the street looked at us too long and I felt my father's entire life tighten in my spine while Amara squeezed my hand and we kept walking; the first time I cooked for her, no raisins in the potato salad, God save my soul, and she pretended not to notice that I Googled the recipe twice.

We also had reckonings. The night a patient's family made a comment that was both racial and gendered and violent in the small way that rots you from the edges first, I watched Amara stand there, armor on, voice calm, and do her job anyway. I didn't fix it. I ferried tea, tracked down social work, and stood at her shoulder.

On the Uber ride home, she didn't talk. I didn't press. When we reached my building, she leaned her forehead against my jaw and stayed there until the driver's meter beeped in protest.

"Pineapple?" I asked; our joke turned barometer.

"No," she said. "Just . . . hold." So, I did.

Spring shouldered winter aside. One cool afternoon, she stopped us in the middle of a crosswalk when she said, eyes on the traffic light, "My dad wore a coat like yours the night he told me to choose medicine, not music."

I looked back at her, oblivious to the cars about to blast their horns at us.

"He was already sick." She swallowed. "He loved that I loved both. He said medicine would teach me how the body fails, and music would teach me why it tries not to."

"And you chose one."

"I chose both," she said, surprising me. "I hum in hallways when I'm scared. I never noticed until you started listening and told me."

I reached for her hand. The light changed, and we moved together.

That summer, we hosted a family dinner at her high-rise condo in Harlem. Both sets of parents came, along with Malik and two aunties who'd decided I was acceptable after a round of cross-examination at a recent weekend family dinner.

Amara and my dad stood shoulder to shoulder over the casserole dish. "You're sure about the evaporated milk?" he asked.

"It's not negotiable," she said. "You should know this! Your mom was Trinidadian. And don't stir once it's in the oven."

My mom passed them, playfully slapping his butt. "Listen to her, Marcus."

Amara's mother, Denise, stood beside me, watching everything play out.

"My husband had hands like that," Denise whispered. "Always making, always feeding." She paused, eyes still on my parents with her daughter. "He would've liked this. I think he had a hand in it somehow."

After dinner, Malik clapped me on the shoulder. "You're alright," he said. "The potato salad passed."

We stood side by side, looking over the room. Our parents traded recipes like old friends, while one of the aunties queued music that pulled everyone into a collective sway and head-bob. Amara laughed at something my father said, the sound bright and sure.

I didn't feel like a guest in her world, nor was she a guest in mine. We were both here, standing on the same ground. It all felt less like arriving somewhere new and more like coming home.

Amara came up to me, and I looked down at her, feeling so full. "You good?" she asked.

"Perfect."

By the door hung two black coats: the one that had started everything and the one I'd bought her for her birthday. They rested side by side, ordinary yet astonishing, ready for many winters to come, a quiet code the heart didn't need to page for either of us to hear.

54

What Grandmothers Hold

— ♥ —

The fish vendor squinted at me like I'd lost my mind.

"Mary, gyal, you sure you want this cascadura today?" He held up the silvery creature, its scales catching the morning light like scattered coins. "This one fresh, but you know how long this thing does take to prepare?"

I nodded and count out the bills from my neatly folded household money. Twenty-four dollars. More money than I'd ever spend on fish in a week. Cecil's pension don't go very far. But today was no ordinary day. Today, my son was coming home so I could meet his younger child for the first time.

"Yes, Uncle Benny. It look good."

The bus ride back from Arima did give me time to turn it over in my mind. Five years since Joromi left Trinidad with Margaret, promising to send for Trisha "soon." Five years of watching my husband, Cecil, bite his tongue every time that boy called. Five years of being everything for everybody. Mother. Grandmother. The one holding this whole blasted family together with phone calls, letters, and hardheaded love.

But today was different. Today I finally meeting Heather, my second granddaughter. She was the child I only know from photos. I study that little face in every picture Joromi send, hunting for any piece of us in her. I used to dream about grandchildren running up and down my yard, fighting for my lap, calling out, *Granny!* Life hand me something else altogether, yes. Two grandchildren separated by an ocean, one I'm raising and one I'd never held.

By the time I reached home, the sun was rising behind the mountains, and Trisha was bouncing on her toes in the gallery, wearing the pink dress we'd ironed together the night before. Her hair freshly braided into two puffs, still tie down with that bright silk scarf, making her look like a tiny old lady. I couldn't help but smile.

"Granny!" She rushed to me as I climbed the front steps. "You ready to see Daddy and meet my little sister?"

That excitement in her voice seize my heart. For weeks, this child had been practicing imaginary conversations with her father. She decided she would call him "Daddy Joromi" since she had always called my husband, her grandfather, "Daddy." Now she was planning games to teach Heather, stories to share, and little ways for a big sister to make a little sister feel welcome.

"Let me pass, chile. I have to cook," I said, lifting my market bags over her as I stepped around and into the house.

Cecil was in the kitchen, already dressed but moving slowly, the way he did when his mind was heavy. He caught my hand as I set the bags on the counter, pulling me close despite my protests.

"Cecil, I have things to do . . ."

"I know, I know." His arms circled my waist, his chin resting on my shoulder, but I could feel the tension in his body. "But first, tell the truth. How yuh feelin' about today?"

I let myself lean back on his chest, just for a moment. Forty-two years now, and his body still know exactly how to hold mine.

"I'm nervous," I tell him. "What if Margaret feel like I trying to outshine her? What if little Heather don't take to us? What if . . ."

"What if that boy shows his face here, acting like father of the year?" The words came out sharp, bitter. Cecil's arms tightened around me. "Five years, Mary. Five years of every other Sunday phone calls and broken promises. And now he want to parade his new family in front of Trisha like—"

"Cecil." I turned in his arms, placing my palm against his chest. He asked me how I was, but he was the one with something on his mind. His heart was racing.

He closed his eyes, jaw working. "I know. I know I'm supposed to be . . . Ah trying, Mary. But every time I think about him coming here, I just . . ." He broke off, stepping away from me, hands clenched at his sides. "That's my granddaughter playing down this corridor. My granddaughter . . . because we're the ones who . . ." His voice cracked.

"Come here." I reached for him, and he came reluctantly, letting me hold him this time. "You have every right to be angry."

"Do I? Because everybody expects me to be the bigger man. To welcome him with open arms. To pretend like . . ." He pulled back, wiping his face roughly. "I'll be good, Mary. For you and for Trisha, I'll bite my tongue. But don't ask me to be happy about it."

The following hours passed in a familiar rhythm. Trisha helped me in the kitchen, her small hands eager but careful as I showed her how to arrange the red hibiscus from our yard. It was her special touch for her father's welcome.

"You think Heather is going to like it here, Granny?" she asked, adjusting a bloom with serious concentration.

"I'm sure she will, baby. And she's going to love having a big sister like you."

What I didn't tell her was how my heart was hammering against my ribs every time I thought about the afternoon coming. I felt it then, that old weight on my shoulders. I was always the one making everybody comfortable. Smoothing things over. Pulling people into family even when they didn't quite fit yet. And it was on me too, to love all of them enough to make room for whatever mess they bring in.

At one point, Cecil appeared in the kitchen doorway, just watching us work. When I glanced up, he smiled. That small smile he does save for me alone. It ease me, just a little. He moved beside me as I swiveled the callaloo with the wooden stick, his hand find its way to the small of my back, so natural we don't even call it out. I feel steadier the minute he touch me so.

By a little before three, I sent Trisha to wash her hands again. A moment later, Cecil found me in our bedroom, staring at myself in the mirror, fussing with my dress.

"Stop that," he said gently, coming up behind me. Our eyes met in the mirror as his hands settled on my shoulders. "You look good."

"I look old and worried."

"You look like the woman I married. Still taking my breath away." He adjusted the collar of my dress, his fingers lingering at my neck. Then he turned me to face him. "Mary, listen to me. Whatever happen today, we have each other. We have Trisha. We have this life we built. Nothing that boy does or doesn't do can change that."

I reached up to straighten his shirt collar. "When did you get so wise?"

"The day I married you." He kissed me again, slower this time, and I let myself sink into it. Oh, the comfort of his familiar mouth, the solidity of his body, the promise that whatever happened, I wouldn't face it alone.

We stood together in the gallery, both of us watching the road.

The sound of the car engine made my heart skip a beat. Through the gallery rails, I watched a red rental car pull up to our gate. Joromi step out the driver side, taller than I remember, in clothes looking expensive and not-from-here. *Sweet Lord, is this really my boy?*

Margaret was precisely what I expected. As I remembered, she was polished, careful, beautiful. But today she was watching everything a little too hard, like she was bracing for something.

But it was the little girl who tumbled out of the back seat that made me catch my breath. Heather. My second granddaughter, finally here. At two, she clung to Margaret's hand, with all her soft curls and serious eyes reminding me of Joromi at that age.

"Granny?" Trisha appeared at my elbow. "Is that them? Is that my father? Is that my sister?"

"Yes, baby. Come, let's go meet our family."

Cecil squeezed my hand once before releasing me, and we moved forward together.

The next hour go the way these big days does go, everybody trying they best and still not sure what to do with their bodies.

I watched Margaret's careful politeness, the way she moved through my house. She hovered at thresholds, straightening a coaster she wasn't using. She had come often, back when she lived on the island and was courting Joromi, yet even then, and still now, she carried herself like a stranger. Nothing like Trisha's mother, God rest her soul, who used to move through this house like it was hers from day one.

I saw Joromi's nervousness in the way he kept clearing his throat, his hands restless as he tried to figure out how to be a father to one daughter while meeting the other for the first time. And under all of it was that old thing between him and Cecil, like it never really heal up. There was a stiffness that never seemed to leave him, worsened by all the years he'd been physically and emotionally absent from our lives.

Across the room, I caught Cecil watching me. When our eyes met, he gave me that slight nod. *You doing good,* it said, and I felt my shoulders relax.

But mostly, I watched my granddaughters discover each other.

Heather stayed close to Margaret's side at first, thumb in her mouth, but when Trisha offered to share her homemade doll, Ruby, with its brown skin and yarn hair, the toddler's face lit up. "Dolly!" she exclaimed, reaching out with eager hands.

"Yes, baby," Trisha said patiently. "Dis is Ruby. You can play with her."

When we sat down to eat, I served each dish with extra care. Cecil sat at the head of the table as always, but his leg pressed against mine underneath. It was a grounding touch. Margaret was gracious, asking questions about the recipes and complimenting the flavors. Heather ate quietly, making little sounds of pleasure at the cheesy macaroni pie, but was mostly content to stay on her mother's lap.

When Joromi complimented the food, Cecil's hand found mine beneath the table, squeezing gently. We'd cooked this meal together, me preparing the fish with Trisha in tow, while he made the curry, our bodies moving around each other in the practiced dance of a shared kitchen and a shared life.

After the meal, while I was gathering the plates, Joromi approached me in the kitchen. This was the first time we'd been alone all day.

"Ma," he said softly. "The food was perfect. Just like I remembered."

I paused in my movements, studying his face. He looked older, more serious than the boy who'd left. "You remember your grandmother used to make that same curry sauce?"

"I remember." He leaned against the counter, and in that moment, he looked so much like Cecil.

"Ma, I want to . . . I need you to know that I appreciate everything.

What you and Daddy did, taking care of Trisha. I know it wasn't easy."

"She's not a burden, Joromi. She's your first blood."

"I know that. But I also know what you gave up for her. The move to St. Croix, your plans . . ." He faltered. "I failed her, Ma. Failed you both."

Before I could respond, Cecil darkened the doorway. I hadn't heard him coming, but I recognized the set of his shoulders, the way he held himself when trying to contain something explosive.

"Failed?" Cecil's voice was dangerously quiet. "That's the word you choosing?"

Joromi straightened. "Daddy, I . . ."

"No." Cecil stepped into the kitchen, and I saw Joromi instinctively back up. "You don't get to come in my house, eat at my table, and talk about failure like it's something in the past. Like it's something you can apologize away over curry and rice."

"Cecil . . ." I started, but he held up a hand.

"You failed? Present tense, boy. You failing. Right now. Every day that child wakes up asking why her father doesn't call more. Every birthday you miss. Every time she sees other children with their fathers and I have to watch her face . . ." His voice broke, anger crumbling into something rawer.

Joromi's face had gone ashen. "Daddy, I'm trying to . . ."

"Trying?" Cecil laughed, but it was harsh, bitter. "You know what trying looks like? Trying is your mother plaiting Trisha's hair for school every Sunday night. Trying is me, in my old age, stepping up to guide a little girl through things no man ever taught me to explain. Trying is . . ."

"That's enough." I stepped between them, my hand on Cecil's chest. I could feel his heart pounding, see the moisture in his eyes that wasn't quite tears. "Both of you. That's enough."

"I need some air," he said roughly, and turned to leave. At the doorway, he paused, not looking back. "Your daughter is in the living room, Joromi. Your firstborn daughter. Maybe you should go talk to her instead of standing here discussing your failures."

Suddenly, Cecil turned back and gestured to his son, "Yuh know what . . . Come. Let's take dis outside."

My stomach clenched. I didn't follow. A woman knows when to step in, and when to hold the line and let men sort out their own mess.

Through the kitchen window I watched them under the mango tree. Cecil's hand was on Joromi's shoulder, their heads bent close in conversation. Sap sweetened the air; a kiskadee called from the fence. Joromi gestured, clearly emotional. Cecil shook his head, then pulled our son into an embrace. When they came back inside, Cecil caught my eye and gave me the slightest nod. *We'll talk later*, it said. *It's going to be okay.*

Meanwhile, I took the opportunity to speak with Margaret. I found her in the gallery, watching the girls play.

"Margaret," I began gingerly, "I want you to know how grateful I am. For taking care of Joromi, for raising Heather so well, for . . . for sharing her with us today."

"Mrs. Enoch, I need you to understand something." Her voice was gentle but firm. "This visit is important, and I want the girls to know each other. Joromi and I are really focused on our lives in New York right now. Trisha . . . she's happiest here with you. This is her home."

I hear what she really saying under the nice-nice. *Don't get ideas, Mrs. Enoch. Don't read more into it than a visit.* I coulda get vex. Part of me wanted to. But as I looked at this young woman, protective, guarding her territory while still allowing this connection. I recognized it. The way she stood just a little closer to Heather. The way her hand never quite left her back. That same fierce thing that made me take in Trisha without question. How could I fault her for that when it was the same instinct that made me take in Trisha's mother years ago?

"I understand," I said. "But Margaret, you must understand too. Trisha is a part of all of us. She carries Joromi in her smile, she carries my mother's stubbornness, she carries this family's blood. Distance don't change that."

Margaret nodded slowly. "I know. And I'm not trying to take that away. I just . . . I need you to know where my boundaries are."

"Boundaries," I repeated, testing the word. "Yes, I suppose we all need those."

As the afternoon wore on, I noticed Cecil growing quieter. He'd stationed himself in Trisha's room, listening to the girls play but not joining in. I was just about to suggest we serve tea when I heard it. The soft grunt came from the hallway where Cecil stood. His hand went to his chest, fingers pressing hard against his shirt. I was at his side fast, tilting my head further down the hallway toward our bedroom. He hesitated, that stubborn pride flaring, but another wave of discomfort crossed his face and he moved.

In our bedroom, away from the others, his facade crumbled.

"It's nothing," he said, but he sat heavily on the bed, one hand still pressed to his chest. "Just . . . indigestion probably."

"Cecil Enoch, don't you dare lie to me." I sat beside him, taking his wrist to feel his pulse. It was rapid. "Is it your heart?"

"No." He shook his head, but caught my hand, holding it tight. "It's . . . I don't know. Everything just feeling tight. Can't breathe proper." His eyes met mine, and I saw the fear there. "What if it's . . . Mary, I can't. Not today. Not with them here."

I know it then. Not heart attack. This was panic. Fear tightening him up from inside. My strong husband, the one who does hold up everything, was breaking down under the weight of this day.

"Look at me," I said firmly, cupping his face. "Breathe with me. In . . . out . . . that's it."

"I can't go back out there." His voice was small, so unlike him. "I look at that boy and I want to . . . And Trisha trying so hard to impress him, and that woman acting like we're . . . like we're just . . ."

"Shh." I pulled his head to my shoulder, feeling him shake. "It's alright. You don't have to be strong every minute."

"Yes, I do." The words were muffled against my neck. "You need me to be. Trisha needs . . ."

"What I need is my husband, not some superhero." I pulled back to look at him. "You think I don't see? How you bite your tongue till it must be bleeding? How you hold all this anger so I don't have to? Cecil, you're allowed to be human."

He laughed, watery and weak. "You wait till my knees start creaking to tell me that, eh?"

I helped him lie back on the bed and loosen his collar. "Rest here for a few minutes. I'll tell them you're checking something."

"Mary . . ."

"No arguments." I kissed his forehead, tasting salt. "Let me take care of you for once."

When I returned to the living room, I made Cecil's excuses smoothly. But Trisha, perceptive as always, sidled up to me.

"Where's Daddy?"

"He's just fixing something, baby. He'll be back soon."

She studied my face with those too-knowing eyes. "Is he upset? Because of Daddy Joromi?"

I smoothed her hair, this child does see plenty. "Sometimes grown-ups have complicated feelings, sweetheart. But your grandfather loves you more than all the stars."

"I know," she said simply. "That's why he's upset."

By evening, his breathing had eased, the tightness gone from his shoulders, and he drifted back to us.

The afternoon unfolded in carefully managed conversations and brief pauses. I made sure Trisha had time with both her father and her sister. All the while, I felt Cecil tracking me. His glance from across the room when Margaret said something that he knew would grate on my spirit. His hand brushing mine as I handed him his cup of hibiscus tea. The way he stayed close whenever I looked like I might need backing. And I understood that he was not only watching over me; I was looking over him, too. He was leaning on me, too.

As the sun began its descent toward evening, the inevitable moment arrived. I hold onto Joromi with that desperate mother love because I know I might not see my son again for years. Margaret's embrace was brief and perfunctory. When I lifted little Heather for a goodbye hug, she pressed her warm cheek against mine and patted my shoulder with her tiny hand. That small thing was so sweet it nearly crack my heart open.

And Trisha . . . my Trisha stood straight and tall, smiling as the red car pulled away, waving until it disappeared around the bend. Only then did she let her carefully maintained composure crack.

"Granny," she said, her voice small but firm as we walked back into the house. "I hate red now."

"Is that so, baby?"

"Yes." She yanked the remaining ribbon from her hair, the other having gone missing in all the excitement. "Red is a lying color. It pretends to be pretty, but it just goes away."

Cecil knelt down beside me as I gathered Trisha into my arms.

Together, we held her, our granddaughter, our girl, as she finally let herself cry.

"You know what I learned today?" I said softly. "I learned that love is bigger than distance. Heather loves you already. I could see it. And your father, he loves you too, even if he doesn't know how to show it properly."

"But they went away, Granny. They all went away and didn't take me!"

Cecil stood; his hand touched the back of my neck and rubbed, a calming touch, just for me. "Trisha, sweetheart," he said gently. "You know why they didn't take you?"

She looked up at him, tears streaking her face.

"Because you belong right here with us. And we're not letting you go anywhere."

That night, after I'd tucked Trisha into bed and listened to her prayers, I found Cecil in our bedroom. He was sitting on the edge of our bed, already in his pajama bottoms, his shirt unbuttoned.

I moved to the dresser and began removing my jewelry. The earrings first, then the necklace Cecil had given me for our thirtieth anniversary. In the mirror, I watched him watching me.

"How you think it went?" he asked.

I sat beside him, and immediately his arm came around my shoulders, pulling me close. "It went like family, I suppose. Messy and beautiful and complicated."

"And Trisha? How's our girl?"

"Trisha is going to be fine. She is stronger than all of us, I think. And she got something now she didn't have before. She has a sister who loves her, even if they are far apart."

"Come here," Cecil said softly, shifting so I could sit between his legs, my back to his chest. His hands found my hair, carefully removing the pins I'd forgotten, working through the style I'd so carefully arranged that morning. This was our ritual. After tough days, after family drama, after anything that left me wound too tight to relax. His fingers in my hair, patient and gentle, until I could breathe again.

"What did Joromi say to you?" I asked. "Out there under the tree?"

Cecil's hands paused, then continued their work. "He wanted to know if we thought Trisha would be better off with them. If maybe it was time."

My whole body went rigid. "And what did you tell him?"

His arms came around me, pulling me back against his chest, his lips close to my ear. "I told him that child is exactly where she's supposed to be. That we are not giving her up. That he had his chance to step up five years ago, and he chose differently. That don't mean he can't be her father, but Trisha is ours now. She's home."

I rose and turned in his arms to face him, my hands framing his face. "Cecil Enoch, I love you so much sometimes it scares me."

He smiled, that slow, warm smile that still made my heart skip after all these years. "Good. Because I am not going anywhere." His thumbs wiped away tears I hadn't realized were falling. "We're in this together, remember? For better or worse? Through everything?"

"Through everything," I said, nodding.

He kissed me then, soft and deep. When we finally pulled apart, he rested his forehead against mine.

"You did well today, Mrs. Enoch. Held everything together like you always do. Kept me in line, too."

"You're lucky I love you, or I'd let you run wild."

Cecil let out a deep laugh that warmed my chest, and I couldn't help but join him. Our shoulders shook together, the years between us folding into that easy joy we'd built.

We got ready for bed in the comfortable silence of a long marriage. He brushed his teeth while I changed into my nightgown; I turned down the bed while he checked that all the doors were locked. When we finally settled under the sheets, I curled into his side automatically, my head on his chest, his arm around my body.

"Cecil?" I whispered into the darkness.

"Mm?"

"You think we're doing right by her? Taking her dreams and keeping them small, keeping her here when maybe out there . . ."

"Stop." His hand found mine, lacing our fingers together over his heart. "You're not keeping anything small. You are the one giving her roots. You give her love. You're giving her a home she can always come back to, no matter where life take her. That's not small, Mary. That's everything."

I listened to his heartbeat.

lub-dub

lub-dub

lub-dub

His fingers traced lazy patterns on my arm, a touch so familiar it was like breathing.

"You remember when Joromi was small?" I asked. "How we used to dream about what kind of father he would be?"

"I remember." His voice was soft in the darkness. "But that boy turned into a different man than we imagined. Doesn't mean we love him less. Just means we love different than we planned."

"We've had to do a lot of different than we planned, haven't we?"

He shifted, turning onto his side so we were face-to-face. "Mary, look at me." In the dim light from the window, I could just make out his eyes. "If somebody had told me four decades ago that this is where we would end up, raising our granddaughter in our retirement, watching our son choose his new family over his first, I don't know if I would have believed we could do it. But here we are. And you know what?"

"What?"

"I wouldn't change anything. Not if it means losing one day with you. Not if it means losing Trisha. This life we built, even with all the heartbreak, even with all the disappointments, it's ours. And it's good."

I kissed him then, pouring into it all the gratitude and love I couldn't quite put into words. His hand slid into my hair, and for a few moments, we were just Mary and Cecil again. Not grandparents, not disappointed parents, just two people who'd chosen each other and kept choosing each other through everything life threw at them.

When we finally settled back down, his arm tightened around me. "Get some sleep, love. Tomorrow's a new day."

"Tomorrow we help Trisha write her first letter to Heather."

"Tomorrow," he agreed, his lips brushing my forehead. "But right now, just rest."

Outside, the evening chorus of crapauds and crickets began their nightly song. Down the hall, I knew Trisha was sleeping with one arm wrapped around her doll, the other stretched across the pillow where dreams could hold all the conversations she'd planned to have.

And somewhere between New York and Port of Spain, a plane carried my son toward his chosen life.

But here, in this bed, with Cecil arm around me and my granddaughter safe down the hall, I feel that earlier panic ease off me, little by little. The fear that had gripped me in the kitchen, that terrible moment when I thought Joromi might take her away, felt distant now. It dissolved with Cecil's words, Margaret's boundaries, and the simple truth that Trisha was ours to love and protect.

"I love you, Cecil," I whispered.

"I love you too, Mary. Always have, always will."

The kitchen is clean, and my granddaughter is safe in her own bed where she belongs. Cecil's breathing deepens beside me, his arm still around me even as sleep claims him. I let my hand rest over his heart, feeling its rhythm, this heartbeat that has been the soundtrack to my adult life.

As sleep comes on, I think about the love that does travel, and the love that does stay. Love that leave, and love that does sit down right here and hold me. Not the big beginning, but the middle. The arms that catch you when you wobble. The voice that tell you, *we in this together*, and mean it, same way it mean breakfast and bills and locked doors.

I whisper the same words I'd spoken over my son when he was small: "Sweet dreams, baby. I love you."

But this time, Cecil's arm tightens around me in his sleep, and I know the words are for both of them. For the child down the hall and the man beside me. Joromi has taken root in another land, and I no longer wait for the cascadura to call him back. Some stories don't end with anybody coming back. They end with you letting go.

Love on the Fourteenth Floor

The elevator chimed on the fourteenth floor. Marcia shifted from one Birkenstock slipper to the other. Her heart hammered against her ribs like a hummingbird trapped in a cage.

After she made no move to exit, he said, "This is us."

She looked up and saw that the elevator was indeed on the top floor.

But then, instead of her legs moving, her mind caused words to tumble out in a breathless rush.

"Hi!" she yelled, her voice betraying a nervous hitch. "I'm Marcia, your . . ." Her voice trailed off, searching for an excuse, any excuse, to get a conversation started.

"I'm Jeffrey."

Neither of them moved.

The mechanical doors dinged and began to close. She slapped the "open" button with enough force to impress a bouncer. His thick eyebrows tilted up. He stepped out first. His locs flowed, his blue eyes sparkled, and his shoulders looked sculpted for slow-motion walks. He turned left, flashed a small smile, and disappeared.

For several seconds, her eyes watched him go, then Marcia did not float. She bolted. She had to tell Talia. *I met him!* Earlier that week, she and her best friend had noticed his name in the updated resident directory. A new tenant on fourteen, it read in neat block letters: JEFFREY NOAH.

She hurried down the narrow, dim hallway on the fourteenth floor. The carpet was worn thin in the middle from years of use. She passed her door and the laundry room, heading straight for Talia's.

She knocked hard. "Talia, open up. I need a witness."

Silence. Nothing. She pulled her preppy cardigan across her chest as a chill swept over her.

She knocked again. The sound carried farther than she intended. "Girl, I have data to report."

She checked the knob. Locked, of course. She pulled out her phone and called.

Two rings. Voicemail?

She tried calling again. "Pick. Up."

Voicemail.

A trickle of unease slipped into her chest.

A neighbor wheeled a trash cart past. Marcia offered a polite smile but kept her eyes on Talia's door like she could summon her by glare alone.

She called a third time, whispering, "Tee, stop playing."

Voicemail recording again.

The smile of the guy she met in the elevator faded into the

background. Talia never let Marcia's calls go unanswered. Even during a migraine, she once picked up and whispered, "Speak soft or die." They built their friendship on terrible timing, shared snacks, and immediate pickup etiquette.

She knew something was off.

Marcia pressed her forehead against the door. "Where are you?"

No answer. She walked back toward her apartment.

Then she made a decision. Not a wise one.

A *Marcia* one.

She turned and walked down the hall to her best friend's apartment. Crouching, she peered under the door. She searched the narrow ribbon of light for a shadow, a footstep, or anything that showed the silence was a choice, not an accident. The tile felt cool against her palms and emitted a faint smell of bleach. There was no motion in her friend's apartment.

That was when Mrs. Henley from 14B rounded the corner and gasped.

"My God, Marcia, are you breaking in?"

"I'm checking on my friend."

"You look like someone failing a burglary class."

"Please," Marcia said, standing. "If I were burglarizing, I'd wear black."

"You are wearing black."

Marcia paused. Looked down. She was, in fact, wearing black leggings.

"Well, I didn't plan that."

Mrs. Henley patted her arm and shuffled away, mumbling, "These young people."

Marcia sighed and called again.

Voicemail. She usually never, ever left voicemail messages. She hated the sound of her voice. But she made an exception today.

"Talia, hi. I tried knocking. You aren't here. Where are you? Please call me."

She straightened. "Fine. I'm getting chamomile," she said to no one.

Chamomile helped her think. It kept her from spiraling, and from kicking Talia's door off the hinges.

She turned toward her own apartment, but her phone buzzed in her hand before she took two steps. A text from Talia.

At the clinic. Appt ran long. Do not panic.

Marcia texted back right away.

You missed my call. Have you been kidnapped?

No. Calm down.

Impossible. I need context.

Tired. Running behind. Be home soon.

Marcia stared at the screen, reading between every line. *Clinic? What for?*

Talia never used short sentences. Talia texted like she was writing her debut memoir.

Something was very wrong. Marcia continued to her apartment and went in this time. The air greeted her with lavender from the diffuser and the faint memory of yesterday's takeout.

She'd often kick off her heavy slippers, drop her bag, and sink into the worn center of her sofa.

Today, she leaned her back against the door. With the focus of a secret keeper, she listened closely. Each time footsteps approached, she pulled the door open.

First came old Mr. Vernon, the super, from 14H, shuffling toward the elevator in his plaid pajamas. He noticed her standing stiffly in the doorway and gave a suspicious squint. "You checking for ghosts?"

"No, sir," Marcia said.

"Good," he replied. "They don't pay rent, and I don't have the energy to evict 'em."

He shuffled on.

A teenage boy appeared at the end of the hall. He was a bit darker skinned, around thirteen or fourteen, with narrow shoulders and long arms. He held a slice of pizza halfway to his mouth. He froze when he saw her staring directly at him.

"Uh . . . hi?"

"Not you," Marcia said.

He held up the pizza. "Okay, but . . . you're kinda creepy."

"Eat your food."

He backed away slowly, never breaking eye contact until he got to his apartment door.

Talia appeared seven minutes later. Her bookshop tote bag was slipping off her shoulder. She had the look of someone who had wrestled a long day and come in second.

"Tee," Marcia said, stepping forward.

"Hi," Talia breathed out, the word barely formed.

"Hi? That's all I get?"

Talia opened her mouth, closed it, then sighed. "Girl . . . I am . . .

exhausted."

She shuffled by Marcia with a tired nod. Marcia stepped in line behind her as they entered Talia's apartment.

"What happened?"

"It was supposed to be a quick checkup. Then bloodwork. Then a new nurse seemed determined to turn my mother's arm into a juice box."

"Oh, you were at the clinic with your mother? Why do you look so pale?"

"I am always this shade."

"No. You look like almond milk today."

Talia snorted. "I hate you."

"Very mutual. Let me help you."

Inside Talia's apartment, Marcia moved on instinct. Jacket hung. Bag set down. Shoes off and placed in the short white credenza. This place was usually very neat. Counters were wiped down, lights were low, and it felt orderly and calm.

But today, *oh my* . . . Plastic cups were scattered across the island and sink. Crumbs covered the counter. Talia had dropped her clothes in the hallway, like signals left behind.

Keeping her eyes on Talia, Marcia poured water into a clean glass.

Handing the glass to Talia, she asked, "You hungry?"

"No."

Marcia ignored that. She opened the cabinets. She found crackers, peanut butter, and a pack of emergency mango slices. The dehydrated fruit was expensive and therefore sacred, but the moment demanded it.

Talia curled up on the sofa, slowly lifting her feet onto the ottoman.

She moved like someone who had battled gravity all afternoon.

Marcia sat beside her. "Talk."

Talia shook her head.

"Talk," Marcia repeated.

"It's not serious."

"You texted me like a hostage. Start explaining."

Talia hesitated. "I've been going to the clinic more. My mom's lupus is getting worse. I'm coordinating her care. Trying to cover the bills she can't. And work started cutting our hours again. So, I've been picking up shifts at that awful bakery with the dry croissants."

"You're doing all of this alone?"

"I didn't want to bother you."

Marcia blinked. "Bother me? I just tried to break into your apartment."

Talia laughed for real then, head tipping back, hand clutching her stomach. It came out of her in a soft, raw burst. It was the kind of laugh that appears after a long day when you really need a bright moment.

"You should have seen me, Tee. I was on the floor like a spy from a B-rated movie."

"Were you checking the vibe under my door?"

"I looked insane."

"Well, you are insane."

Relief spread across Marcia's face as she smiled at her friend. The sister energy between them was solid and familiar. She scrutinized Talia's face and thought, *She's holding more than she's saying.*

"I can help with your mom. She loves me. Why didn't you tell me?"

"Because you always have so much going on."

"No. I always have so much dramatic nonsense going on. You're allowed to interrupt the nonsense when serious things rise up. That's what friendship is."

Talia whispered, "I didn't want to be a burden."

Marcia squeezed her hand. "Girlfriend, we're meant to share these burdens. True friends support each other."

Talia released a loud sigh and leaned her head on Marcia's shoulder. "I'm tired."

"I got you."

Marcia gently guided her down, cradling her head and easing her onto a pillow. Once Talia settled, Marcia stood and moved around the apartment. She picked up stray cups and tossed a load of laundry into the hamper. She swept the crumbs off the counter. She made a low, steady sound under her breath. Not cute. Grandma energy. Purposeful.

When she returned, Talia had dozed off. Marcia nudged her knee. "Eat the mango."

Talia half-opened her eyes. "That is my emergency stash."

"This is an emergency," Marcia said. "Eat."

Talia obeyed, nibbling dramatically as if she were receiving communion.

When the sugar hit, her eyes opened fully again. "Thank you."

Marcia settled onto the sofa. "I met the new resident in the elevator, Tee. He was f-ine."

She smiled, recalling how it all began. She had rushed down the hall, eager to share everything.

"I was coming to you to gossip, you know. That was the plan before I discovered you went completely off grid."

Talia lifted an eyebrow, eyes twinkling, and waited for more.

"This guy," Marcia continued, warming to it, "had a smile that could charm a snake. Full of confidence, like he knew exactly what it did to people. And the locs," she said, shaking her head. "They fell down his back like a midnight waterfall. I swear the elevator got smaller around me just to make room for him."

Talia snorted. "I hate when that happens."

"And his eyes, girrrl," Marcia went on. "They were this deep blue, like reef water on a perfect day. So weird for a Black man. He must be mixed. His eyes widened when he caught me staring, as if he was surprised to see me there." She paused, then added, quieter but amused, "I think they got darker."

"Stop," Talia said. "You ran, didn't you?"

"I absolutely ran," Marcia admitted. "I stuttered, panicked, bolted, and decided you needed to hear about it immediately."

She looked at Talia then, the way her shoulders sagged, the way exhaustion blanketed her face.

"And now," Marcia said, softer, "I'm glad I came."

Talia sighed and tucked her feet under her. "I should have said something sooner."

"You will tell me from now on . . . please."

Talia nodded slowly.

They sat together in an easy familiarity, the kind that didn't need fixing.

Later, they migrated to the fire escape with blankets, mugs of tea, and the leftover mango slices. The city stayed busy below. Marcia rested her head on Talia's shoulder; Talia bumped her back with hers.

A person walked a dog across the street. The dog wore a tiny sweater that looked like a big knitting project.

Talia pointed and cackled. "That dog is dressed like a church usher."

Marcia wheezed with laughter. "He looks like he collects tithes."

A tall figure crossed the block. Even from their high spot in the building, he looked like a heartthrob from a steamy romance novel cover. His thick locs moved with him.

"Yummmm," Talia murmured.

Marcia let out a quiet snort. An hour ago, she was breathless for him. Now, she finds it funny how quickly everything can change.

"Yes, girl. That's Jeffrey, the elevator god I was telling you about."

Jeffrey looked up as if he sensed they were talking about him. He saw Marcia on the fire escape and waved.

Talia elbowed her. "Call down and ask him to get coffee with you."

Marcia shook her head. "No. I'm busy. I'll be busy."

Talia tapped her chest. "Busy with me?"

"Exactly."

Tonight belonged to the woman beside her. Talia was not okay, and Marcia had to be the one to help her. This was the pact they never had to say out loud.

For a few moments, they both grew quiet.

Then Talia said, "You know we are absolutely ridiculous."

"Fully."

"And codependent."

"Only a little."

"And dramatic."

"You say that like it's a bad thing."

They laughed loudly, sipped their tea and shared snacks. Marcia and Talia invested time in a friendship that mattered.

This, too, was love.

The Affair She Didn't See Coming

— ♥ —

Return to Source

By the time Renee spotted the flyer, she had already decided her body was the enemy.

It was taped to the glass door of a smoothie shop on Peachtree, wedged between a lost-cat notice and a gig poster. The heading was printed in thick maroon letters.

RETURN TO SOURCE: A Sensuality and Soul Workshop for Women

Breath. Body. Ancestral Wisdom.

Midtown Atlanta. Saturday evenings.

Renee read it three times, then pretended she had not, then snapped a photo anyway.

Behind her, Tanya slurped the last of her pineapple ginger smoothie. The straw rattled against ice. "You are not taking another picture of a sign," Tanya said. "Please tell me it is not another declutter-your-closet challenge."

Renee slid her phone into her cross-body bag. "It is nothing."

Tanya raised one perfectly drawn brow. Her freckled face always made her look amused, even when she was annoyed. "Your voice got that guilty wobble. Let me see."

"No."

"Yes."

Renee sighed and handed over the phone. Tanya glanced at the photo, then at her friend. "Sensuality workshop. Okay, I am listening."

"It is probably a scam," Renee said. "Somebody charging nine hundred dollars for breathing."

Tanya grinned, slow and wicked. "First of all, Atlanta will absolutely charge you nine hundred dollars for breathing. Second, when was the last time you thought about sensual anything that did not involve DoorDash?"

A group of Georgia Tech students brushed past them on the sidewalk, laughing too loud. A MARTA bus groaned by, a cloud of heat and fumes in its wake. Midtown slugged along around them, glass towers, food trucks along 10th, a rainbow crosswalk in the distance.

Renee tugged at the hem of her T-shirt. It read, in peeling letters, **I GOT OUT OF BED FOR THIS**. Her leggings cut into her stomach a little. She had planned to start a new workout program last month, then the breakup had knocked the air out of her.

"Hardy and I were together for four years," she said. "I do not think my first official act as a single woman should be humping the air with strangers."

Tanya's face softened. "You are not humping the air. You are reclaiming your body."

"You read that off Instagram."

"And yet I am right."

Renee looked away, toward the flat Atlanta sky, washed pale over the buildings. Her hands itched for something to do. She twisted the silver ring on her pinky, the one her therapist called her "fidget ring." The ring helped when her brain felt like a crowded room, everyone talking at once.

She had a hidden diagnosis now, stamped in black ink on her chart: ADHD, inattentive type. It made sense of the half-finished projects on her laptop, the laundry forgotten in the machine, the way her attention snapped to sounds then could not find its way back. Hardy used to joke that her mind lived in three tabs at once. He stopped joking when the bills went unpaid.

"It is not just the breakup," Tanya said quietly. "You have not looked comfortable in your own skin for a long time."

Renee swallowed. Midtown lights flicked on, one by one, a soft grid against early dusk.

The workshop title echoed in her mind. *Return to Source.*

She heard her grandmother's voice, faint yet firm, drifting from those childhood summers in Tobago. "Your *okra* is your soul, Renni. No matter what this world tells you, that part of you is from Nyame. Untouchable."

Back then, she'd thought Grandma meant okra, the slimy vegetable she pushed around her plate. Years passed before she discovered the truth: **okra,** the Akan word for the divine spark planted in every soul before birth. The part of you that no one could steal.

As for **Nyame**, that mystery lingered even longer, a word that tasted of reverence on her grandmother's lips but remained undefined in her child's mind. Not until much later would she understand.

Tanya's voice cut into her reverie. "Renee, you must do this! Shall I do it for you?"

"Fine," she relented without too much fuss. "Send the email. If it is weird or culty, I am blaming you forever."

Tanya clapped her hands. "I already texted them. There was a QR code on the bottom."

"You are evil."

"You are welcome."

***

The studio sat on the third floor of a brick building off Peachtree Place, squeezed between a Pilates studio and a law firm. Inside, the air smelled like orange peel and something earthy, like rain on warm dirt.

Renee paused at the door, pressing fingers into the soft place just above her hip bone. Her stomach fluttered. Group spaces made her nervous. Too many bodies, too many noises, then the rush of the air from the cooling unit would fuse with someone's laugh, and her brain would slide sideways.

She checked that her phone's captions were enabled, just in case. People thought she was rude when she tilted her ear toward them and asked them to repeat. The audiologist had called it a "mild processing issue," nothing dramatic enough for a hearing aid. To Renee, it felt like words sometimes arrived late, the meaning trailing behind the sound.

"Ren," Tanya whispered, bumping her shoulder. "You are doing great. You look cute."

"Cute is a strong word."

Her reflection in the glass door showed a short Black woman in dark green leggings and a soft black tank. Her teeny-weeny afro was dyed a deep indigo-black with constellation patterns shaved into the sides: tiny stars that caught the light when she turned her head. Silver ear cuffs climbed up both ears like armor. A mark curved along her jaw from childhood stitches when she fell headfirst onto her aunt's glass living room table. Her lips, full and bare, pressed together.

Tanya swung the door open.

The room was expansive, warm, and low lit. Amber lamps sat in corners. A circle of floor cushions surrounded a shallow altar in the middle, carved from dark wood. On it sat a white cloth, a bowl of water, a small brass figure of a well-endowed woman, and three candles that burned with calm blue flames.

A woman in a long dark green dress moved through the space, adjusting cushions. Her locs were threaded with thin gold beads, and the gray strands caught the light. A faint limp marked her walk, one foot dragging a fraction, but her presence filled the room.

"Welcome," she said. Her voice, with a quiet certainty, was accented in a way that clipped certain consonants and elongated others. "I am Akosua. This is Return to Source."

Tanya mouthed, "She is fine," then widened her eyes like a cartoon.

Akosua smiled, as if she had seen. "We will begin in a few minutes. Make yourselves comfortable. Shoes off, phones on silent. If you need to step out at any time, do so quietly. This is a space of choice, not pressure."

Renee liked that sentence. *A space of choice.* She chose a cushion slightly off-center, not at the far edge but not in the direct line of the instructor either. Tanya sat to her left, already untying her sneakers and wriggling toes with chipped red polish.

Women trickled in, a mix of ages and bodies. A tall woman with an undercut and gold hoops. A soft-spoken auntie type in a floral kaftan. A younger woman with a cane tucked carefully beside her cushion, lipstick the color of ripe plums.

Renee's heartbeat tried to sync to the low drum track playing from a speaker. Boom, pause, boom. Her mind drifted to Hardy, to how his hands moved across her skin with the frantic precision of someone defusing a bomb, methodical yet racing against time. She missed being touched. She did not miss the way he sighed when she forgot to text back or lost track of time.

"Close your eyes," Akosua said when everyone had settled. "Place one hand on your heart, one on your belly. Feel the weight of your life right here."

Renee obeyed. Her palms felt hot against her T-shirt.

"In my tradition," Akosua continued, "we say you have *okra, sunsum,* and *honam*. Soul, spirit, and body. Your okra came from God before you took your first breath.

The word hit Renee like a physical force. *Okra.* Her grandmother's voice bloomed in the darkness, faint yet firm: *Your okra is your soul, Renni.* The hand on her heart slipped to the floor and gripped the mat's edge. She had to anchor herself to the present even as the past rushed through her.

"Your sunsum is your personality, your energy, the way you move through the world. Your honam is the body that carries all of it. Many of us learned to love others before we were taught to love any part of ourselves."

Renee's throat tightened. She kept her eyes shut. In the dark, the room became sound and warmth and heartbeat.

"Tonight is about remembering," Akosua said. "Not performing. Not being sexy for anyone's gaze. It is about coming back to your own."

Renee shifted, aware of the soft give of her belly under her hand. She had spent years sucking it in, hiding it in high-waisted jeans. The idea that it might deserve tenderness felt almost obscene. She remembered then to raise her hand back to her heart.

A timer chimed softly.

"We will work with partners in this series," Akosua said. "For safety and focus, you will not see your partner's face. You will hear them. Feel them through their words. You will send and receive through voice notes and prompts during the week."

Renee's eyes flew open.

Tanya glanced at her, then at Akosua. "So like a phone relationship?" she whispered.

"More like a mirror with a heartbeat," Akosua replied, as if she had heard the comment. "Your partner will not be in this room with you. You will be paired through our app. No photos, no social media handles, no names if you choose. Only voice, breath, truth."

Renee frowned, her instincts prickling a warning.

"Our system listens for themes in what you share, so it can reflect your words and energy back to you in ways that support your growth. Nothing leaves this space."

"What if my partner is a creep?"

"You set your boundaries," Akosua said. "You end any exchange that feels wrong. We moderate. We listen. And remember, this is for you. Not for them."

Renee nodded before she could stop herself.

Akosua gestured to a low table near the wall, where tablets lay in neat rows, each with a pair of over-ear headphones. "At the end, you will record your first message. A simple introduction. Your sunsum, speaking to someone who wants to know you without seeing you."

Renee's skin prickled. The idea of someone hearing her before seeing her made her want to crawl out of her body and also stay right where she was.

"Let us begin with breath."

By the time the session ended, her limbs felt loose, as if someone had unknotted cords she did not know were tied.

They had breathed in counted patterns. They had rolled their shoulders, circled necks, pressed fingers into tense jaws. At one point, Akosua had them stand and sway with eyes shut, following the drum, hips moving slow. Renee had kept her movements tiny, afraid to be seen, then realized no one was looking at her. They were all busy trying to *feel* themselves.

Now the group sat in a crescent while the altar candles burned steady.

"You have done well," Akosua said. "Now you will meet your partner with your voice."

She nodded toward the tablets. "Choose any station. You will see a question on the screen. Answer it with honesty. Thirty seconds or three minutes, it is up to you. This will be the first thing your partner hears from you."

Renee wiped her palms on her leggings. Her heart restarted its busy pounding. She stood when Tanya nudged her.

"Let us get you a mystery lover," Tanya murmured.

"Stop," Renee hissed, eyes smiling.

"Fine. A mystery . . . growth opportunity."

Renee snorted, which helped.

She chose a tablet near the corner. The screen glowed with a simple prompt:

Tell your partner one thing you have forgotten about your own body that you want to remember.

Her throat went dry.

She slipped the headphones on. The world narrowed to the screen of the device and her own breath in her ears.

A red circle waited on the screen. She stared at it for a long moment. *She hovered, thumb trembling, trying to decide if this was brave or foolish.* Half a second later, she tapped.

The Opening

"Hi," she began, then winced at how small the word sounded.

She gathered herself, lowering her shoulders. "My name is Renee. And the thing I have forgotten about my body is that it used to feel like home."

The sentence hung in the silence.

Her voice thickened. "I forgot that it once felt good to exist inside myself. Before I started treating my body like a problem to solve or a chore to manage. I want to remember what it feels like to touch my skin without flinching." She paused. "That's it."

Her thumb hovered over the stop button. She exhaled and tapped.

The recording uploaded with a soft chime. A message flashed: Your partner will receive this within the hour. Expect their introduction by morning.

Renee's chest tightened in anticipation and dread. She removed the headphones, placed them gently on the table, and walked back to her cushion. Tanya grinned like she was watching the season finale of a drama.

"How was it?" she whispered.

"I might vomit," Renee whispered back.

Tanya squeezed her knee. "Perfect."

Renee waited until she was home to check her phone again. Her apartment sat on the corner of Juniper and 5th. A slim Midtown walk-up with creaking steps, a view of the parking lot behind a Thai restaurant, and hardwood floors that looked better in low light.

She tossed her bag onto the couch, kicked her shoes off, and found herself pacing. The city's soundtrack played low and constant. A siren somewhere distant. The continuous, low whirr of the building's central fan. Someone's dog yapped twice and fell quiet.

Her brain rustled through thoughts like papers in a wind current.

She forced herself to eat something, heating sweet plantains and leftover rice. Her fork clinked against the plate. She managed three bites before giving up and washing her hands under the faucet to reset.

Then her phone buzzed.

You have received a partner introduction.

Her heart banged once against her ribs. She wiped her palms on her shorts and tapped the notification.

A blank screen appeared, nothing but a single audio file.

She pressed play.

A low breath filled her ear. Smooth. Unhurried. The voice that followed defied gender, sliding gently through the speaker, warm and silky, like someone speaking to her from across a candlelit table.

"Hello. I am your partner."

Renee blinked. The voice also didn't sound any specific age. It had a careful softness people used when they did not want to startle a skittish animal.

"I listened to your message," the voice continued. "You said your body used to feel like home. That stayed with me."

Renee pressed a hand to her chest.

"I want to share something too," the voice said. "I have forgotten how comfortable I used to feel with my own breath. Somewhere along the way I started holding it, like I was bracing for something. I want to remember how my breath felt before fear got there first."

They paused, as if choosing their next words carefully.

"I look forward to learning with you."

The recording clicked off.

Renee stared at the screen long after it went dark.

She replayed it twice, then set down the phone as though it were a fragile artifact.

She slid onto her couch, pulling a blanket over her lap. Her fingers traced idle patterns against the soft fabric. She hadn't expected to feel anything. Not over a stranger's voice. Not this soon.

But the voice had landed somewhere deep, the same way music sometimes vibrated through her bones. It felt personal, like the person had spoken directly into a quiet room inside her.

She closed her eyes. For the first time in months, the tension in her jaw loosened.

The next session took place a week later.

Renee reached the building early, partly to avoid the crush of women arriving at once and partly because she needed a moment to center herself. Midtown was thick with late afternoon heat. Sunlight bounced off mirrored glass towers and spilled across the street like molten gold. Sweat collected along her hairline.

Inside the studio, the air felt cooler than last time. The lamps cast soft pools of amber against the walls. A gentle instrumental track played, deep flutes alongside slow drums.

Akosua stood near the altar, adjusting a bowl of water. She lifted her head the moment Renee entered. Her gaze carried a quiet intensity that made people stand straighter without being told.

"Good evening, Renee," she said.

Renee startled. "You remember my name?"

"I remember the way people carry themselves," Akosua replied. "Names follow after."

Renee nodded, unsure how to respond. She settled onto a cushion near the middle this time. Women around her murmured greetings, settling in with water bottles and folded blankets. Tanya arrived a minute later, breathless and radiant as always, sliding into place beside her.

"Your partner message came yet?" Tanya whispered.

"Yes."

"And?"

"Weirdly nice."

Tanya grinned. "I love this for you."

Before Renee could respond, Akosua raised a hand.

"Tonight," she said, "you will listen to a new message from your partner. You will also move through a guided exercise that may feel familiar and unfamiliar at the same time. You must remember, this work is not about performing sensuality for anyone else. It is about learning the shape of your own presence."

She struck a small brass bell. The sound shimmered through the room.

"Let us begin."

The exercise started with breath again, then with touch. Not sexual, not performative. Simple contact. The instructor guided them to place their palms on their ribs, then trace the lines of their shoulders, then hold the back of their own necks as if comforting a younger version of themselves.

Renee's hands shook at first.

Her ADHD mind zipped from sensation to sound to the faint vibration of the floor when someone shifted. She breathed through it, grounding herself by pressing her feet into the mat.

"Now we introduce the voice," Akosua said.

Tablets were handed out again. Renee sat with hers on her lap, her reflection faint in the black screen.

"Your partner has left you a prompt," Akosua explained. "Open it. Let your body respond as it will. Do not force."

Renee tapped the screen.

The voice from last week emerged, warm as before, a little lower than she remembered.

"Hello," they began. "My question for you is this. Where on your body do you feel forgotten? Place your hand there now."

A strange heat unfurled across Renee's collarbones.

She placed her palm on her left shoulder. The spot always hurt after long days, a knot behind the joint that pulsed when she was stressed.

"Stay there," the voice said. "Notice warmth. Notice absence. Notice whatever rises."

Her shoulders softened, her sitting bones sinking into the cushion.

The voice continued. "Now breathe into that place. Even if it feels strange. Even if you feel silly. Just breathe."

Renee closed her eyes and followed.

For a moment, the studio faded. There was only the rhythm of her breath and the stranger's voice threading through her awareness.

The closest thing to defining what happened next was that she cracked open.

She didn't cry. But the space inside her, crowded for months with noise, quieted enough for one clear thought to surface.

I want to know this person.

Not romantically. Not yet. But intimately. With curiosity. With the hunger of someone who had been numb for too long.

Her fingers curled gently against her skin.

And for the first time, she wondered what it would feel like to be held by her own touch without apology.

The Revelation

The messages became a rhythm.

Every few days, a new voice note appeared in the app. Each one carried a prompt or a reflection, never longer than three minutes, always ending with a pause that felt like an open door.

"Tell me about a time you felt powerful in your body," the voice would say. Or "Describe the first touch you remember that felt kind, not just functional." Sometimes they simply described breathing, slow and patient, as if modeling how to inhabit a moment.

Renee answered more than she meant to.

She recorded in her bedroom, the one with the crooked blinds and the plant that refused to die. She recorded in her car, parked under a tree on Peachtree Place, traffic whispering by. Once she recorded sitting cross-legged on her living room floor, back against the couch, feeling the grain of the hardwood under her thighs.

She tried to keep her answers neat. Safe. Then, her body betrayed her.

"Once," she heard herself say one night, "I felt beautiful in a way that scared me. I was dancing at a party in Trinidad. The music vibrated through my ribs. My dress stuck to my back. I caught my reflection in a glass door and thought, that woman looks alive. I have not seen her in years."

She stopped the recording, cheeks burning. Then she hit send.

The reply came the next morning.

"I hear you," the voice said. "You sound alive even when you are remembering. Maybe that woman is closer than you think."

The comment should have rolled off her. Instead, it settled in her rib cage like a small, warm stone.

By the fourth week, Renee knew a few things about her partner.

They favored slow, measured speech. They often flipped her words back to her, not mocking, more like holding up a mirror. They rarely shared details about themselves, but when they did, they landed with precision.

"I used to move like I did not want to take up space," they admitted once. "Now I practice walking as if the ground is lucky to feel my weight."

Renee laughed out loud at that, alone in her apartment. She practiced the same thing on the sidewalks of Midtown later that day. Chin a little higher. Shoulders less clenched. Feet hitting the pavement like they belonged.

Some nights she fell asleep with the earbuds still in her ears, her phone screen gone dark, the last note from her partner echoing in her head.

Tanya listened to about two sentences from one of the recordings before waving her hands. "Okay, I get it," she said. "Hot in a weird therapist way."

"It is not hot," Renee said, although it was, in a quiet way that made her knees soften.

"It is fine," Tanya said. "You are allowed to be turned on by someone who respects your nervous system."

Renee rolled her eyes, but she replayed that line later. *Turned on by respect.* The idea delighted her, really.

Week five brought a new exercise.

Akosua dimmed the lamps lower than usual. The studio seemed steeped in a heavier-than-usual silence. Everyone seemed more settled, less fidgety, as if the group had agreed to trust the floor.

"Tonight is about sight and touch," Akosua said. "You will work with a mirror. You will listen to your partner while you look at yourself. If you need to avert your eyes, do so. If you can keep your gaze, even better."

Assistants passed small standing mirrors around the circle. Renee set hers on the mat in front of her and adjusted the angle.

Her reflection stared back. Indigo coils. Her jawline scar, some would call a keloid. Soft belly under a loose tank. The starry design on her scalp had grown out a bit, and a few stars blurred into new shapes.

She fitted the headphones over her ears and opened the app. A new message waited.

"Hello," her partner said. "Tonight I want you to look at yourself while you listen. You do not have to like what you see. You only have to agree that this is you."

Renee swallowed. She held her own gaze, mouth pressed tight.

"Notice one thing that intrigues you," the voice continued. "Not something you want to fix. Something that draws your attention."

Her eyes dropped to her collarbones. The skin there was a shade lighter than her face. A small mole sat just above her right collarbone, dark against brown.

"I am looking at a mole," she whispered, forgetting for a second that the recording was one-way. "I like that it looks like a dot of onyx paint."

The voice went on. "Now imagine that every mark on your body is a sentence in a story. Some sentences hurt. Some are funny. Some are boring. They are all yours. And, Renee, you do not have to erase them to move forward."

Her name in that voice, this being the first time they'd said it, sent liquid heat pooling low in her belly. Her thighs clenched involuntarily, a pulse of want so unexpected she nearly gasped. She pressed her palms harder into the mat, trying to ground herself against the sudden ache between her legs.

The unexpected arousal collided with something deeper, something raw. Renee's throat tightened. Her eyes blurred. She blinked hard, refusing to let tears fall in a room full of strangers.

The voice softened. "Will you consider, for tonight, that your body is trying to fulfill you, not ruin you?"

The recording ended. Silence rushed in.

Renee exhaled, a long release that trembled through her ribs. The silence that followed felt thick, almost warm.

Her awareness crawled back into her body piece by piece. The weight of her legs folded beneath her. The slight tremor in her hands. The heat lingering between her thighs. She blinked, and the studio swam back into view.

Women around her were in their own worlds. One wiped her cheek with the heel of her hand. Tanya, a few places away from her, sat perfectly still, eyes closed, breathing slow. A soft sigh came from the far side of the circle, as if someone had finally loosened a knot they'd been harboring.

Renee searched their faces, just long enough to see that no one looked shocked. No one looked embarrassed. And no one was looking at her. The room held a shared, quiet knowing. Whatever happened in her body was not strange here.

She lowered her gaze to the mirror again. Her reflection stared back, cheeks flushed and eyes unwavering. The mole above her collarbone looked darker under the low light, a small mark with more history than she had ever given it credit for. She touched it.

She wasn't curious about this experience anymore. Curiosity felt too light for what stirred within her. She felt present. Rooted. As if she had slid back into herself after years of hovering somewhere just above her life.

A soft movement broke her focus. Akosua stepped into the center of the circle, her shadow brushing the altar's edge. She didn't speak immediately. She only looked at them, each woman in turn, as if she could see what they had just confronted.

When her gaze reached Renee, she gave the slightest nod. A recognition. A blessing.

Then Akosua spoke, her voice like honey folding into warm butter.

"You met yourself tonight. More than you realize."

Renee froze for a second, the meaning slipping just out of reach. *More than you realize.* It echoed in her mind. *What did that mean?*

***

The invitation to the last session arrived on a Wednesday morning.

CLOSING RITUAL: MEETING YOUR MIRROR

The email included instructions. Wear something comfortable. Be prepared to listen. Be prepared to choose.

Renee spent way too long picking an outfit. She settled on black joggers and a soft burgundy wrap top that crossed at the front and tied at the side. It showed a hint of cleavage when she moved, which she tried not to think about. She looked at herself in the glare of the bathroom mirror as she slipped silver cuffs onto both ears and traced a thumb along her chin before leaving.

The sky over Midtown was streaked with orange and gray as she walked. Cars inched along Peachtree beside her. A group of teens took photos at the rainbow crosswalk, posing and laughing. A man in a suit jogged past them, briefcase in hand, earbuds in, face set.

Renee's heart beat faster the closer she got to the studio.

Tanya met her outside the building. "You look like a goddess," she announced. "A slightly terrified goddess, but still."

"Thanks. I think."

"You ready to see your mystery person?"

Renee hesitated. The thought sent a sharp thrill through her, part anticipation, part fear. "Yes," she said finally. "Whatever happens, I am ready."

Inside, the layout had changed.

The cushions were arranged in a wider circle. Against the far wall stood six folding screens, simple wood frames with opaque white panels. A seventh space sat empty, no screen at all, only a full-length mirror framed in dark wood.

The altar remained at the center, candles now joined by a small clay pot that smelled faintly of smoke and herbs.

Akosua waited beside the mirror. Tonight she wore a deep green dress that matched the color of pine needles after rain. The limp in her walk was more noticeable as she stepped forward, but it did not diminish her presence.

"Welcome to your closing ritual," she said. "You have spent weeks speaking into the dark. Tonight we invite light into the room."

Renee's stomach flipped.

"You may be wondering if your partner is in this space with you physically," Akosua continued. "Some of you may imagine a face. A body. A story. Tonight, you will meet the source of the voice that has been walking with you."

She gestured to the screens. "Some of you will choose to meet someone on the other side. Some of you will choose the mirror. Both choices are valid. Both are encounters with yourself."

Whispers rippled through the room.

Renee's gaze locked on the mirror. Her palms dampened.

Akosua's eyes swept the circle. "Before we move, I need to tell you something about this work. When you registered, you were asked to upload a series of private voice notes and reflections. Some of you make voice memos already. Some of you recorded just for this program. With your consent, our system listened. It pulled phrases, tones, rhythms, and built a companion voice for you."

Renee's next inhale came after too long a pause and her eyes widened in disbelief.

"In other words," Akosua said gently, "much of what you have heard these weeks has been you."

The room went very still.

Renee's mind raced back through the messages. The careful way the partner repeated her words. The phrases that sounded oddly familiar. The feeling that this person knew how her thoughts moved before she finished speaking.

A low murmur rose, different reactions overlapping. Surprise. Recognition. A few soft curses.

Akosua continued. "The voice you received blended your own speech with a trained guide. It was never a random stranger. It was your okra and sunsum speaking to you in a form you could hear. Not everyone is ready to know this. You are."

Renee closed her eyes.

Her first reaction was irritation. She had poured raw pieces of herself into those notes, believing another human being was holding them. There was comfort in that idea. A witness. A possible lover. The promise of being chosen.

But under the sting sat something else: a quiet, fierce relief.

If the voice was her, then someone had been listening to her all along. Not Hardy. Not Tanya. Not even Akosua. Her.

"You may still choose a screen," Akosua said. "You may want to sit with another person and share what you learned. Or you may choose the mirror and meet yourself, with this knowledge. Either way, this is your final act in this series."

Renee opened her eyes.

Tanya nudged her. "We can go to a screen," she whispered. "Or I can guard the door while you run."

Renee almost laughed.

Instead, she stood.

Her legs carried her toward the center of the room before she made a conscious decision. The mirror waited, reflecting candles, cushions, and a dozen blurred shapes behind her.

She stood in front of it and met her own gaze.

Her reflection looked winded. Eyes bright. Mouth slightly parted.

The scar on her jaw curved like a comma, a pause rather than an ending.

Akosua's footsteps approached, slow and even. She stopped at a respectful distance away.

"You chose yourself," she said softly.

"I thought I wanted a stranger," Renee replied. "I thought that would feel more exciting."

"And now?"

Renee studied the woman in the mirror.

"Now it feels like I have been flirting with myself for weeks," she said. "And I did not even notice."

Akosua smiled, the corners of her eyes crinkling. "That is one way to describe a reunion with your own soul."

Renee snorted quietly. "Feels like an affair."

"With who?"

"With the part of me I abandoned."

Akosua inclined her head. "Say something to her then."

The room faded, just for a moment. It was Renee and the woman in the mirror.

She lifted her right hand. Her reflection mirrored her. They touched palm to palm against the cool glass.

"I am sorry I treated you like a problem," she said. "You carried me anyway. You kept breathing even when I held my breath. You deserve better from me."

Her eyes stung. She let the tears fall this time.

"I want to learn how to love you without waiting for someone else to go first," she whispered.

Her reflection's face crumpled and steadied in the same instant.

Behind her, she sensed movement, the quiet shift of bodies, the soft murmur of other women speaking to each other or to themselves.

Akosua's voice floated gently to her. "Your okra has been waiting for those words."

Renee laughed through the tears, short and shaky. "Feels late."

"Your soul does not keep score," Akosua said. "It waits."

Renee looked at herself one last time, seeing every mark and curve with a tenderness that felt like love beyond first glance.

Later, she would walk out into the thick Atlanta night with her shoulders less hunched. She would cross the street like the ground was lucky to feel her weight. She would get home, stand in front of her bathroom mirror, and touch her own face as tenderly as she had always wished someone else would.

For now, she stood in the studio, palm pressed to glass, at the end of the first true affair of her life.

Not with a stranger.

With the woman she was finally ready to love.

The Affair She Didn't See Coming

Under Long-Term Observation

The last stroke of ink bled into the paper, and the lawyer cleared his throat.

"That completes it," he said. "You are now legally divorced."

Nancy set the pen down carefully, as if she were placing a glass ornament on a thin shelf. She patted the instrument twice with her left hand then clasped her hands together on her lap again. On the surface of the table, the black barrels of their pens rested parallel, a neat little symbol of a thing that had never stayed straight for long.

"So, this is it?" Bill asked.

His voice sounded almost curious, as if someone else had spoken and he was waiting to see what she would say.

"Yeah," she said, not looking at him. Her gaze held fast to the documents, to the version of herself she had learned to pass as, typed out in capital letters. **NANCY A. SHAW.** The last name she had accepted when she married Bill.

Her first name was not the name her grandmother had whispered over her crib. That name, honoring her Indian ancestors, faded away in elementary school. Teachers struggled with it, and classmates turned it into a mockery. Nancy had been a compromise. Easier for everyone.

"It's time," she added.

Bill leaned back in his chair and ran his index finger along the edge of the table. The movement looked idle. It was not. He was testing the grain, feeling the drag on his skin, grounding himself the way he always did when something important deviated.

"I really thought we would make it to ten," he said, lying.

"Ten was never our number." Her eyes, the color of burnt molasses, flicked to him then before returning to the papers.

He waited in the silence. The lawyer shuffled pages and pointed to the last signature lines. They signed again. Their names settled in ink, side by side for the last time.

When it was done, Nancy pushed her chair back. It scraped against the tile, a harsh sound in the neat little office.

"Thank you," she said politely to the lawyer, because manners sat on her tongue even when her life splintered. Outside in the hallway, she waited for the elevator without looking at Bill. In the reflection of the doors, she watched herself instead, a woman who no longer moved like time was on her side. Short curls. Dark honey-brown skin that pointed to her Indian and African lineage. Eyes that glowed when she was young, but not anymore.

She blinked a few times and made a silent promise to herself as the doors opened. *I will be joyful again!*

On the sidewalk, the sunlight felt heavy and bright. City noise wrapped around them. She gave him a small, tight-lipped smile, something like gratitude, something like apology.

Then, she said, "Take care, Bill," turned away and let him go.

He wanted to say her real name in that moment. The one on the long-ago birth certificate. The name he had heard only once. She shared it with him during a fevered night when it felt she gave herself to him completely. He never said it since and at this juncture, he felt like he shouldn't be caught with those syllables.

"You too," he said.

She turned away, her figure swallowed by glare and movement. He watched until the crowd closed around her and there was nothing left to see.

Yes, he thought. Seven was always our number. Not ten. Not forever. Seven.

***

The apartment felt devoid of her. No shoes by the door. No bottles crowding the bathroom sink. No faint soca music drifting from the kitchen.

Bill stood in the entryway, absorbing the quiet. To most people, it would have felt empty. To him, it felt clean and uncomplicated.

Now, he said it. "Nayantara . . . Nayantara!" He unleashed her name into the space, imagining it splashing onto the walls, permeating and becoming.

He went first to the kitchen. To the cabinet over the stove where the mugs were stored. There were five plain white ones that they had chosen together, and the space where the blue mug used to sit.

SHIDENI GROUP.

In his mind, the image of that mug rose clear, its gold block letters burned into memory. He recalled the first time he took it down and hid it elsewhere in the apartment. The fight that followed. The way her voice lifted as she insisted the missing mug meant nothing, that it was just a thing. The lie lingered between them and unsettled him because Shideni was not a random company. It was her ex's. He first learned of him in the background check he ran the night they "met." He had not moved the mug to punish her. He had moved it to observe her. To see what she would do without it. Whether she would panic. Whether she would confess.

She had done neither. She had gone quiet. Slept on the very edge of the bed for three nights. Then, on the fourth morning, she acted as if nothing were wrong. By then, he had returned the mug to its place. The relief in her eyes when she opened the cabinet had been slight but unmistakable.

People revealed themselves when the right objects were disturbed. He had learned that long before he met her.

"So, you took your boyfriend's mug," he mused.

Bill closed the cupboard and stood still for a moment, listening to the apartment, listening for what might not fit. Pipes ticked. Somewhere below, a door slammed.

He moved then, going from room to room, gathering the things she had "forgotten" to take. He carried them all into the spare room. In the theory of their marriage, it had been his home office. In practice, it was a staging area. Nothing personal stayed visible there.

He crossed to the desk and unlocked the bottom drawer, pulling out a black box. He set the box down first, squared it with the edge of the desk. Using the code of their marriage month and day, he opened the combination lock and pulled the top wide open. The burner phones were where he had left them. The thumb drive lay parallel to the file folders, its metal edge catching the lamplight. He picked up and unfolded a photograph of a much younger version of himself standing beside a woman whose face had been carefully burned away.

He laid down her satin scarf, smoothing the fabric once before folding it. A notebook where she wrote short stories and notes from her people-watching followed. He placed a single wooden earring, featuring an Akoma symbol, in the corner. This way, it wouldn't scratch the nearest phone's screen.

When he closed the drawer, he checked the lock twice. Not because it might fail, but because habits mattered. Things stayed where they were put unless someone moved them.

That was how you knew where to look.

The words that defined his life before her—cover, mission, tasking, debrief—came back as naturally as breath.

He had tried to live without this work of contract killing for a while. For her. Or that was what he liked to think. The truth was, he had been tired. Seven years of marriage gave him plausible deniability. A traceable life. Tax returns. Couple photos. Witnesses who would swear he was boring.

Now that shell had been legally cracked.

He sat in the desk chair, turned on the small lamp, and powered up one of the phones. No contacts appeared when the screen came alive. He typed a code into the calculator app instead. A different interface slid into view.

One new message.

"Status?"

He looked at the single question for a long time, then replied.

"Cover dissolved. Subject at liberty."

The typing dots pulsed. Then came the answer.

"Proceed with long-term observation. No contact."

He smiled. That part made him feel almost sentimental.

They still did not understand. They thought the marriage had been a strategy, nothing more. A convenient shield. A way to disappear in plain sight.

They were not wrong. Not completely.

But somewhere between the party where he met her and the morning he watched her cradle the mug that she said meant nothing, something changed in him. She had stopped being only a subject. She had become a fixed point in a life built on disappearing acts.

And over time, that felt less like love and more like she was his possession.

***

Three weeks after the divorce, Nancy sat cross-legged on the floor of her new studio apartment, sorting her mugs.

"You would think I was setting up a museum," she muttered, half amused, half exhausted.

Her friend Anaya lay sprawled on the mattress that would eventually become a bed once the frame arrived. "You always were sentimental about cups," she said. "Remember when Mr. Jeffers broke your little ceramic one in Form One, and you did not talk to him for a month?"

"He called me 'Anansi' instead of my name."

"Everyone called you that."

"Exactly." She put another mug aside. "Another reason to leave it behind."

She did not say which "it" she meant: the childhood, the marriage or the mug.

She meant the man who had insisted on introducing her as "Nancy" even after she had told him her full name. He had repeated it once, mouth shaping each syllable, then nodded.

"I do not want to insult your grandmother by mangling it," he had said with a small smile. "Tell me when you are ready for me to use it."

He never asked again.

Now, in the small studio with its peeling paint and stubborn radiator, she tried to think of herself by her original name. She practiced it in her head like a private prayer. She had even written it on a sticky note above her new desk, the full, flowing thing no receptionist ever got right.

Nayantara.

"Earth to you," Anaya said.

"Sorry. Just thinking."

"About him?"

"About me. After him." She forced a smile. "Different thing."

Anaya's gaze softened. "I'm so sorry I introduced the two of you at that lame party. But now, you are out. That is what matters."

Nancy nodded. It was true. No more walking on eggshells around his moods. No more negotiating whether they would see her friends. She stopped adjusting her tone, fearing he might slip into that cold silence. It made her feel like she had lost an important part of herself.

Outside, a siren wailed. Inside, the heater hissed when it came on, shaking the old pipes. The apartment still didn't feel like home. To her, it felt like a waiting room.

She picked up the blue mug with the fading gold letters and studied it. SHIDENI GROUP. She should have thrown it out years ago. Should have left it behind in the old place with the white plates and the heavy pots Bill liked. Instead, she had wrapped it in sweaters and carried it with her, as if it were special.

"Keep it," Anaya said. "It's a trophy, don't you think? Proof that you survived them. The boy. The husband. The version of you that let both of them take up that much space."

Nancy laughed, surprised. "That's dark for you."

"Truthful though." Anaya rolled off the bed. "Order food. I will help you unpack those books next."

Later, when they were eating takeout from foam containers, Nancy glanced at the time. Seven eighteen. She felt a small twist of irritation and spoke before she could stop herself.

"He used to watch the clock all the time," she said. "Bill. Sometimes I would catch him staring at the microwave display like it was a window."

"Was he anxious?" Anaya asked around a forkful of rice.

"No. That was the strange thing. He did not look worried. More like he was counting down to something only he knew."

"You are free of his weirdness now," her friend said firmly. "Let the clock be the clock."

Nancy nodded but somehow did not believe it.

***

A little over a week into the new apartment, she noticed the plant.

The pothos plant on the windowsill had drooped after the move; its leaves had been limp and dusty. She had meant to water it when she finished unpacking. She had not.

That morning, it looked firmer. The soil was dark and damp. A faint ring of moisture stained the saucer.

Nancy poured coffee and stared at the houseplant, its vines spilling over the shelf, leaves glossy, reaching out and toward the ground.

"Did you water this?" she called.

Anaya walked out of the bathroom, a towel around her long, straight hair. Her light-brown Indo-Trini face looked open and unguarded. The scent of Dove soap lingered on her skin.

"No. You did last night."

"I did not."

Her friend shrugged. "Then you forgot you did. Moving is stressful, girl. Your brain has dropped a few files."

Nancy nodded slowly, but the unease did not leave her. When Anaya left for work and the lock clicked behind her, Nancy set her gaze on the door.

She double-checked the chain. The deadbolt. There was no sign of any tampering. *How was this possible?*

Later, she told herself she really might have watered the plant by accident, tired and half asleep. She had lived with worse logic in the marriage. Small things out of place, explained away. A password changed "by accident." A credit card charge from a city he swore he had never visited.

You are making something out of nothing.

She had told herself that for seven years. She tried to think so now.

***

For Bill, the first seven days after her move were pure observation.

He learned her commute. The path she walked from the train. The bodega where she bought yogurt and plantain chips. The laundromat where she sat and read while the machines shook.

He had always been good at disappearing into the background. As a tall, freckled white man in a predominantly Black neighborhood, he should have stood out. Instead, he mastered the art of being a category rather than an individual. Just another gentrifier. Another quiet man with headphones. Another body in the coffee shop.

People saw types. They rarely saw specific faces unless taught to.

On the seventh night, he used the duplicate key to enter her building. The door locks were old, the kind that believed in themselves more than they deserved. She had always trusted locks. He had trusted nothing that could be opened with a single piece of metal.

He stood in her apartment for less than five minutes. He watered the forgotten plant, straightened the rug by the couch, and admired her mug collection on the narrow kitchen shelf. Only one stood apart, in the back.

SHIDENI GROUP.

He did not touch it.

When he left, he reengaged the deadbolt, finagled the chain with a special magnet, and slid the copied key back into his pocket. His phone buzzed only once that night. A reminder for a different operation, one that would not begin for months.

He muted the notifications.

***

After the plant came the mug.

Seven weeks after the divorce, Nancy opened her cupboard and froze.

Kwame's mug sat in the center of the shelf, turned so the fading gold letters faced her. SHIDENI GROUP. She had placed it at the back. She was sure of it. She had stood on tiptoe and tucked it behind the plain white ones, as if hiding evidence.

The mug was a relic from another life. From Kwame. He had worked at Shideni then, all restless ambition and soft laughter, a man who talked about futures as if they were wide and waiting. He had been careless in ways Bill never was, emotionally available in ways Bill could not be. Kwame asked questions. Bill gathered answers. Kwame dreamed in public. Bill observed in silence.

She had kept the mug not out of longing, but out of habit. A leftover artifact from a time before her life had been edited down to fit a marriage. It meant nothing now; she had told herself. Less than nothing.

Yet here it was, pulled forward into the light, its placement too deliberate to be accidental. The shelf had been rearranged with intention. Not carelessness. Not coincidence.

Her pulse climbed her throat.

Someone had been in her kitchen.

Someone who knew exactly which object to move.

She felt as if invisible fingers tightened around her throat. The apartment felt smaller, the air heavier.

You moved it, she told herself. Maybe during cleaning. Maybe while looking for something else. People misremember things all the time.

She picked it up, gingerly set it in the sink and backed away until her butt hit the counter.

Control your breathing, she commanded herself. Panic will not help.

She had learned that with Bill. When he went distant, her fear only deepened the silence. Better to stay calm, to gather facts.

She called Anaya at work.

"Do not hang up," she said when her friend answered.

"Are you okay?"

"Did you come by this morning?"

"What? No. I have been at the office since eight."

"Have you ever moved my blue mug?"

"The Kwame one? Your trophy? Absolutely not."

Nancy let out a sound that wanted to be a laugh and failed. "It moved."

"Girl, what do you mean it moved?"

She explained quietly, gripping the phone tight.

"You need to go to the police," Anaya said when she finished.

"And tell them what? That a mug shifted in my kitchen?"

"That someone broke into your place."

"Only, it was not broken into, and they will ask if anything was taken. Nothing is missing."

"You cannot just ignore this."

"I will not ignore it."

I am logging it.

New resolve crept into her voice when she said, "If there is a next time, there will be more to tell."

"That sounds like the start of a horror movie."

"Then I will live like the girl who finally leaves the haunted house," Nancy said. "Not the one who waits around to be proven right."

She hung up and called the super instead. He promised to change the locks the next day.

Later that night, Nancy stood at the bathroom sink, studying her reflection while the tap ran. The mirror was streaked from the move, her face briefly doubling where the glass warped.

She reached for the hand towel, then stopped. The bright patterned one felt too loud in the small room. She folded it and put it under the sink, replacing it with a plain white one from the linen box.

It looked like every other towel she'd ever used in a rental. Forgettable.

She turned off the water. For a moment, she imagined how it must look from outside. A light on. A woman moving. Nothing remarkable.

The thought surprised her with how balanced it felt.

She switched off the light and left the door open behind her.

She sat up late that night, watching the front door until her eyes burned.

No one came.

***

The locks changed. Nancy noted the new keys, their different weight. She slept better for a while. Weeks slid by. She started a new project at work, made new friends at a community center book club,

What he wanted was continuity. Proof that a person could not walk cleanly out of a life that had intersected with his.

That was the real lie of divorce papers. That signatures could cut binding threads.

He finished his coffee and left exact change on the table. As he stepped outside, his phone buzzed.

Need you back in the field, the message read. Window of operation opens in seven days.

He chuckled. "Of course it does," he said.

He typed a single answer.

I will be ready.

Then he crossed the street, knowing the path she always took home. He needed to check in.

***

Nancy did not see him until the elevator doors slid open.

She had chosen the building's side entrance that evening, avoiding the louder main lobby. Her bag was heavy with groceries. Her mind was full of another life, one in which she might move to a different city, change jobs, start fully over. She stepped into the elevator, lifted her finger toward the button, and froze.

Bill stood in the corner, hands in the pockets of his gray coat.

For a moment, they simply looked at each other. The doors closed behind her with a soft thud.

Every safety lecture she had ever heard surged into her brain. *Get out. Press the button. Make a scene.*

Her body did not move.

"Hello," he said. "Been a while."

"What are you doing here?" Her voice did not sound like hers.

"Visiting a friend." He smiled without warmth. "Small world, right?"

The car began to climb. She felt each floor like a punch.

"You do not have friends in this neighborhood," she said.

"Sure, I do. You live here."

"I am not your friend."

"Once upon a time, you were my wife."

Her heart kicked harder. "You signed the papers too."

"I did." He studied her face. "How is the new place?"

The question flattened her. "Get out of this elevator," she said. "Now."

He tilted his head, as if considering a restaurant suggestion. "We are already moving. It would be inconvenient."

She watched the illuminated numbers tick upward from two to three and then to four.

"Did you come into my apartment?" she asked.

He did not answer.

"Did you touch my things?"

His mouth curved slightly. "You always were very attached to that mug."

Ice slid down her spine.

"I changed the locks," she said.

"I know. You used the cheap set from the hardware store on 139th. Good people. Terrible security."

She hit the red emergency button. The car shuddered to a stop between floors. A muted alarm began to ring.

"There," she said. "Now you can leave."

He looked almost impressed. "That is better. I was worried you had forgotten how to push back."

"You are not supposed to be here."

"I am not supposed to be many places," he said. "That has never stopped me."

She stepped to the far side of the elevator, groceries pressing into her hip. "Why are you doing this?"

He leaned against the rail, hands still in his pockets. "I wanted to see how you would live without me."

"You saw. I am fine."

"You are adapting," he corrected. "But you keep the mug. You keep the habits. You even kept the number."

"What number?"

His eyes flicked up to the panel. "Seven."

"You think you own a number now?"

"I think some things follow a pattern whether or not we like it." He shrugged. "Seven days. Seven weeks. Seven months. You noticed."

Her throat worked. "I am calling the police," she said and lifted her phone.

He stepped toward her. Not fast. Not threatening on the surface. Simply closing the distance.

"Tell them what?" he asked softly. "That your ex-husband rode an elevator in his own city? That a mug moved? That a plant did not die?"

His proximity squeezed the air out of the small space. She could smell his cologne, light and clean, the one she had picked out the first year they were married.

"You came into my home," she whispered.

He let his gaze scan on her face. "You are my home."

"Not anymore."

"On paper," he agreed. "Unfortunately for you, life is not paper."

The alarm continued to ring, faint and useless. Somewhere far below, the super was probably debating whether to call maintenance.

"You are scaring me," she said.

"I have not touched you," he replied.

"That is not the same as harmless."

His expression changed, just a fraction. "You really do not understand."

"Then explain it," she snapped. Anger finally clawed past fear. "Explain why you watched the clock. Why you always knew what time it was but never what I needed. Explain why a mug was more interesting to you than an entire conversation. Explain why you volunteered to marry me in two weeks and then spent seven years acting like you were doing time."

He studied her for a long moment, as if choosing what weight of truth she could survive.

"Because I was . . ." he said at last. "I was on assignment when we met," he continued. "Long term, deep cover, boring as hell. They needed me to look settled. Harmless. Married. You appeared at the right party with the right face and the right story. Independent. Rooted. Brown woman with a complicated name who had already learned how to make herself easier for other people."

"What?"

The word left her thin and useless. Her mind snagged on fragments because the whole of it was impossible. *Assignment. Deep cover. Married as camouflage.* Her first instinct was to reject it as madness, a story stitched together to frighten her. Her second instinct, colder and far more dangerous, was to test what he said against what she already knew.

The long absences that never quite made sense.

The way he never spoke about work, only around it.

The clock-watching. The sealed drawers. The questions he asked that sounded casual but landed too precisely.

Her stomach turned.

"You're lying," she said, but the words had no traction.

The elevator cable groaned and it jerked up . . . *Five . . . Six . . .* then stopped.

A quieter voice inside her whispered what the louder one could not yet form. *If he isn't lying, then I never married a man. I married a cover.*

Another thought followed, uninvited and sharper still. *Spies don't hold trophies. Assassins do.*

Her breath shortened. The walls pressed in. The alarm light flickered overhead.

"Assignment how?" she asked, feeling the question betray her. She was no longer disputing the premise. She was interrogating the terms.

The elevator shuddered.

And Bill watched her realize who he had always been.

Tears burned her eyes. "So, the wedding was just camouflage."

"At first." He paused, then added, "Then it became something else."

"What?" she asked hoarsely. "A hobby? A field experiment?"

"A reference point," he said. "Proof that not every life I built disappeared when the job ended. Proof that I could keep something."

"I am not a thing," she said.

"You were never just that," he replied. "You were also data. History. Pattern. You were the one variable I did not discard when the cover dissolved."

"That is not better."

"It is honest."

She shook her head. "You chose me so you could vanish more safely."

"I chose you because you made the vanishing feel less empty," he said quietly. "And because you understood how to edit yourself. That takes discipline. I respect discipline."

The elevator felt smaller by the second. Every word stripped another layer from the years she thought she knew.

"I left," she said. "I divorced you. You signed. Whatever you think you kept, you lost."

He smiled again, the gentlest expression she had ever seen on a man who could probably break lives with a phone call.

"You walked away from a contract," he said. "Not from connection."

"We are not connected."

"You are using the name you buried," he replied, changing the subject. "You are making new friends. You are reading in laundromats and joining book clubs and trying on a different version of yourself. That is exactly what you did when we met. You were always migrating.

I was the constant."

She swallowed back bile. "You do not get to narrate my life."

"I already have," he said. "For seven years, I filed reports that included you. Where we lived. Where we went. How you changed me. You exist in files you will never see, in places you will never reach. You cannot walk out of that. It is written."

"Why tell me any of this?"

"Because you are planning to leave again. New city. New job. New name on the lease." His gaze was almost fond. "You are trying to escape. I thought you deserved to know it will not work."

"Try me."

He studied her, then reached out. His hand paused when she jerked her head away. But he smiled and pressed the elevator's reset button behind her. The alarm cut off. The car jolted and resumed its climb.

"You can run," he said. "You can change your hair and your name and your country. What you cannot change is that for seven years, you were part of something larger than you understood. That is permanent. The marriage ended on paper. The archive did not."

The doors slid open on her floor. He stepped aside politely, as if they were strangers.

She did not move.

"What happens if I tell someone?" she asked.

"Who would believe you?" he asked back. "The ex-husband who watered your plant and rode your elevator is secretly a ghost in government files? They will call it trauma. Paranoia. They will suggest therapy."

He fixed a stoic glare on her.

"I am not here to hurt you," he said. "That would be sloppy. I am here to remind you that leaving me was not erasing me. It was preserving me. You took me out of the field and placed me somewhere safer. Inside you."

The cold in his tone chilled her more than any threat could have.

He stepped past her then, out into the hallway, and walked toward the stairs.

"Do not come near me again," she called after him.

He lifted a hand in a little wave without looking back.

The doors closed on her floor, and she understood with sudden, sick clarity that the seven years had not ended. They had reset.

***

Nancy moved within the month.

She did not tell Anaya the whole story, only that she had seen him and it had shaken her. She picked a new borough, a new job, a new building with better locks and a security guard in the lobby. She packed lightly, leaving behind anything that felt tethered to the old life.

The blue mug went into the trash. She watched the truck take it away.

She began using her birth name only. She gently corrected people until they said it right. For a while this small victory tasted like defiance.

She stopped writing dates on the calendar. She refused to look for sevens.

Sometimes, in the middle of the night, she woke with the feeling that someone had walked through her thoughts. Not her apartment. *Her.* As if memory itself had a fingerprint.

Months passed. One day bled into another. Work, commute, sleep. New friends. New streets.

On the seventh anniversary of her divorce, her landlord told the police she had not picked up her packages in two weeks. A wellness check found the apartment tidy, bed made, dishes clean in the rack. Her phone sat on the counter, battery dead.

The last search on her laptop was for jobs abroad.

The police report used words like "no signs of forced entry" and "no evidence of struggle." Friends described her as tired but hopeful. The file joined hundreds of others under a bland heading.

Missing adult.

***

In another part of the city, Bill sat in a quiet apartment that did not look like theirs and never would. He reviewed an operation file on his secure tablet, the glow painting his freckled face in cold light.

The mission had gone well. Seven days, start to finish. Clean entrance. Clean exit. No civilian casualties. His superiors were pleased.

A notification popped up in the corner of the screen. A public database update. He tapped it open more from habit than interest.

HARRIS, NANCY A. STATUS: MISSING. CASE OPEN.

Nancy Harris? He stared at the line for a long time.

It was not his doing. Not directly. He had not touched her since the elevator. He had not stepped into her new building, had not followed her into the stores where she shopped. The world was dangerous enough on its own. People slipped through its cracks every day without his help.

But still. The timing.

Seven years.

He closed the file and leaned back in his chair. Outside his window, the city glowed, indifferent.

Somewhere in a secure server, reports bearing her married name and his operational code sat in digital drawers. Their story, rearranged for usefulness, would outlive both of them.

He thought of her standing in that elevator, groceries digging into her hip, eyes bright with anger and fear. She had wanted so badly to believe that signing her name on a single line ended something.

It had ended the part she could see.

The rest went on.

He reached for his phone, opened a blank note, and typed one word.

Seven.

He watched the cursor blink, then added another.

Running.

He saved the note and turned the screen face down. The room fell into a deeper quiet.

He was not happy. Happiness had never been a metric that mattered.

He was, in a way that felt sharper and more permanent, satisfied.

Some stories did not end with justice or healing. Some ended with a simple truth settling into place.

You can leave a person. You cannot always leave the version of yourself you became with them.

Bill looked out at the city and let that truth rest inside him, unremitting and cold, like a clock that never stopped.

Nayantara, you and I, until death do us part. But not today. I feel your breath in this world.

***

In the train bathroom, Nayantara studied the woman looking back at her, then began to unmake her. Hair loosened, then reworked. Part shifted. Pins placed with care. Lip color blotted down to something practical.

Be a category. Don't be an individual.

She had learned that from books read late at night, stories about people who survived by becoming paperwork, aliases, routes. She was desperate to be a character who lived knowing that systems hunted people, not patterns.

The jacket she pulled on was not new, but it had been chosen, stitched and altered in borrowed rooms over several months. When she was done, Nay was gone. Antaya remained. The face in the mirror held less softness, more intention. Someone who did not explain herself.

The train rocked forward. Antaya stepped into the narrow corridor between sleeper cars. She glanced at the coach section by a door, with documents pressed flat against her ribs. Sapelo Island waited at the edge of the map, a place people forgot to look toward unless they already knew it was there. She watched stations pass. This was not escape. It was her assignment. She breathed, counted exits, and measured time.

Bill, I hereby sever you and everything that no longer serves me.

The Practice of Love

— ♥ —

Solange's silence was still in the room when my fingers scrolled to "Nate Barton" in my contact list. The phone rang twice before Dad answered the FaceTime call. Morning light spilled across the gallery in San Juan, the shadow of the almond tree trembling across his cheek. A cutlass leaned against the balustrade, and beside it, a red plastic cup half-filled with rum, most likely.

"Keston," he said. "Morning. America keeping you busy already?"

"It's eleven here," I replied. "Same with you, right?"

He grinned. "Yes. *Oui foute*, de sun hot today. Mango trees finally bearing. De Julie sweet too bad this year." He raised his cup. "And I'm keeping hydrated."

Behind me, Solange's slippers were lined up by the door, neat. We exchanged small talk, then he asked, "And how is Solange? I know dem Grenadians know how to keep a home."

I hesitated then continued, "We've had a rough week."

He leaned back. "Marriage will test you. Sunshine today, rain tomorrow."

"We argued," I mumbled. "I told her it feels as though she's cutting me down. Little things, one after the other. Small wounds that keep bleeding."

He whistled. "That is strong talk. What kind of little things?"

"Corrections. The way she tells me how I might do better. She picks at how I speak, what I forget, how I cook. Each one harmless by itself, but together they sting."

"And you think she doesn't love you?"

"I know she does. But sometimes it feels as though her love is trying to change me. And I don't know who I am if I allow it."

Dad studied me. "Perhaps she is trying to help you grow. Or perhaps she is trying to claim you. But ignoring wounds is worse than admitting them. If you face them, they heal."

***

Our fight had started with the peppers. She had chopped them smaller than usual. I had leaned into my need to correct.

"Don't you dare," she said when I reached for the salt. "Taste it first."

I did. The breadfruit was rich, the turmeric deep, pimento rising to the top. It was good. I should have left it there.

"It's good," I said. Then added, "But, it needs more salt."

She put down the spoon. "Would you like to cook it yourself?"

"No."

"You want to cook anything? Something you must watch over, turn slowly, and finish with patience?"

"I work all day," I said.

"So do I."

"And then you call me on the train to remind me I forgot the spinach. Do you know how that makes me look? To those people?" I hated that it mattered. I hated that I cared how strangers sized me up.

Her eyes narrowed. "Keston Barton, which people?"

"Everyone," I said. "At work. On the street. On the train. In the store. And yes, your people, mine. Trinis, Grenadians. You. Everyone watching. Judging."

Her face hardened. "Tell me, what do we make you feel like? Because you're not talking about spinach."

"You treat me like a project, not a husband. The other day, you corrected me about our first date. Does it even matter to the story whether it was Brooklyn or Queens? Do you know how small that made me feel? And then you're always telling me to go back and finish my degree, as if who I am right now isn't enough. As if you don't believe I could ever decide that for myself unless you keep repeating it."

Her shoulders fell. Not anger. It was something closer to weariness. She turned off the stove, placed both hands on the counter, and spoke without looking at me.

"If I stop wanting more of you, you would be more comfortable. If I stop noticing, you could move through this marriage without question, expecting the island norms of man and woman. Is that what you want?" She looked up at me then.

"I want to be a man who don't have to defend every choice. You and your Grenadian family always think you know better than everybody. Maybe you would be happier with someone else who actually fits your standards. Meanwhile, I'm the one carrying this whole marriage on my back."

"Carrying this marriage!? Keston . . ." She blinked away tears. Straightened up, squeezed her already small eyes to thin slivers, and curled her thick lower lip into her teeth, biting. A beat passed as her furious gaze pierced me before she said, "I want a partner, Keston. You want a witness to your struggle."

I felt the truth in her words, but I could not answer. She walked away.

Alone, half-cooked dinner smells invading my nostrils, a singular thought seared through my mind: *Oh shit, I'm becoming Nate Barton.*

Later, I turned the stove back on, finished the dishes, and left her plate on the kitchen counter.

***

On the small iPhone screen, Dad smiled as though I had been brave simply for telling him.

"So, you say and do all dat," he said. "And then what?"

"And then nothing. We haven't spoken since. We've been orbiting each other for two days now."

What I didn't tell him was how deliberate her distance had become. From the first night, she slid to the very edge of the bed each night, waiting for my breathing to settle before she let herself sleep. How last night she ordered that awful Hawaiian pizza from the place we both swore off! She ate alone before I got home. Every move felt like she was choosing anything but me.

He sipped his rum. "You sound like you are in therapy with that 'orbit' talk. Perhaps you should be."

"It helps," I admitted.

"So why not talk to your wife?" He shrugged. "Unless you plan to start over. New York has fresh starts everywhere."

———

"I don't want a fresh start. I want this one."

"Then stop complaining and be a man," he said, half joking, half serious. "My generation didn't have so many feelings. If a woman hurt you, you hardened, or you found another."

"I don't want to be you," I blurted, before I could swallow it back.

He paused, then looked away. "You think I want you to be me? You think I don't know the damage I did? Ask your mother how she looks at me when she passes on the road. Like dog shit to step around."

I softened. "Dad . . ."

He waved it off. "A man plays the hand he is given. You got to America. A good job. A wife who feeds you and speaks her mind. That is a strong hand."

"There's more," I admitted. "When I'm with our Trini friends, sometimes I feel big. As if I can look down. And then at work, I feel small. I carry both versions home, and she gets them at once."

He nodded. "You are learning scale. Only someone who loves you will tell you when you're going in the wrong direction."

"You ever had someone love you like that?"

He considered, staring off. "Once. She told me, 'You're a song with a good hook and no bridge.' She wasn't wrong. I left anyway."

We sat in silence until my phone buzzed. A message from Solange. A photo of the kitchen table: leaves of fresh thyme, a curl of breadfruit skin, a napkin folded neatly. On it, my name. Beneath it, a key I already owned. *What the . . . ?*

Dad caught my expression. "See? She's leaving breadcrumbs. Pick them up."

"After all dem ugly things I said?" I whispered.

"Don't take it back," he said. "Take it forward. Tell her what you fear. Tell her what you want. Don't hide behind dem metaphors you like. Speak plain."

His hand trembled slightly as he lifted his cup, and for the first time, I noticed the small white scars along his fingers. He had a lifetime of unattended wounds.

"Dad," I said. "What does being a man mean to you?"

He looked straight at me. "It means knowing your fear and not making others pay for it. Not your wife. Not your children. It means carrying your own wrongs without building a house on them."

I nodded, the weight of his words heavy but real.

***

That night, I cooked. *pelau* first. It was Trinidad, me, in a pot. Then, breadfruit and pimento cut the way she liked it. My hands moved slowly, carefully, as if the food itself were part of an answer.

I didn't know when she would come through the door, or if I would need to carry the meal to her. But I knew what I would say when she let me close enough to speak.

That I don't want her silence. That I want to be a man she doesn't have to mother, a partner who can bleed and still stand. That I love her. This life we're living is not a performance of marriage. It is a practice.

I caught my reflection in the dark kitchen window and didn't recognize the man looking back. My jaw was locked, shoulders braced for a storm I knew was coming. The heat from the stove rolled over me. I stood there, stripped of the day's pretenses, eyes fixed on the door as if willing it to open.

The rice steamed, the breadfruit softened, and I waited.

I hear the soft click of our front door easing open. When she stepped inside, the air in the kitchen shifted.

She was tiny, but the smallness carried a narrative. A few curls slipped loose against her temples as she twisted up her thick, black hair, shot through with a copper warmth, high. Her face held that impossible mix of her people. I knew the sharp line of her jaw, the softness of her smile, and a fullness in her lips that I never tired of kissing. I couldn't take my eyes off her now. I felt like I was seeing her for the first time again.

My eyes swept down her body. She wore casual clothes, but they looked stylish on her. A fitted cream T-shirt was tucked neatly into olive joggers. A gold anklet caught the light as she stepped out of her sneakers. She smelled faintly of bergamot and the outside air. She looked like someone who had walked the city, walked her thoughts, walked her ache.

She didn't take another step inside or toward me.

I had planned a speech, but the moment I saw her, the words vaporized.

I didn't wait. I didn't think anymore; I just did. I crossed the kitchen in three strides.

She stiffened at the sight of me coming, her eyes widening, jaw softening, her breath lifting high in her ribs. But she didn't step back.

I reached for her.

Not roughly. Not pleading.

Just with the clarity of a man who finally understood his assignment.

My hands slid to her waist. Her body tensed even more, then melted. Her forehead rested on my chest, just above my heart. A small shudder ran through her, as if she'd held her breath since Thursday and could finally let it out.

I curled around her, arms a shelter and apology at once.

Her palms flattened against my chest.

Then, her fingers fisted my shirt.

She pulled in a small, shaky breath.

She didn't speak.

Neither did I.

There was no sound except the soft, wet exhale she tried to hide in my skin and the bubbly simmer of the *pelau* behind us.

I held her even tighter.

And in that wordless, shaking moment, the practice of our marriage started again.

He Did Not Come Back

The Morning

On the morning he died, Kweku woke before his alarm.

Harlem woke with him.

Cold winter light slid across the low ceiling of the small room he shared with his cousin. The radiator knocked twice before settling. A bus sighed along Amsterdam, its brakes releasing a long breath. Someone outside cursed softly as they navigated a patch of ice. A vendor dragged a metal cart toward any street in this crown of Manhattan, the wheels clattering over a cracked patch of pavement. The faint smell of roasted nuts drifted in from a street stall already firing up for the day.

He lay still for a minute, then reached for his phone.

10:02 a.m.

He had time.

He swung two well-moisturized legs out of bed, looked down on his well-pedicured toes, and spread his fingers out to examine his fingernails. He nodded approval. Today, he did not have to spend an extended time in the tiny efficiency bathroom performing his personal grooming ritual.

Kweku incorporated the extra steps after he met Cleolin. That evening, he overheard her.

"If a man does not care for his skin and nails, they have no chance with me," she told her friend. He immediately examined his own hands. Being a chef, he had clean, low-cut nails. His massive hands were manly, but soft and, thank the ancestors, moisturized. Having assured himself that he was presentable, he turned to see who had made such a forceful declaration and was charmed to find a pint-sized South Asian woman, with hair that fell in a dark sheet down her back and a small bindi resting between her brows. She spoke with a serene confidence that didn't match her size.

She laughed at something her friend said, and the sound hit him like someone had clapped near his ear. The laughter rang out warm and clear with a certainty that commanded his attention. Her smile reached all the way to her eyes.

Kweku forgot whatever he had been doing. He stood there with a bag of onions in one hand, staring like a man who had just remembered the name of a forgotten song. Everything about her felt intentional. The way she tucked her hair behind one ear. The way she shifted her weight. The way she lifted her chin before she spoke again.

She glanced in his direction for half a second. That was all it took. A faint, puzzled crease formed between her brows, the kind of look people gave when they sensed they were being observed.

In that moment, he knew. Before a single word passed between them. Before he learned her name or tasted the spice in her cooking or heard the softness that slipped into her voice when she spoke about serving the community.

He knew he would spend months finding reasons to stand near her.

Love at first sight was not what he believed in.

Not until that night at the summer charity ball he catered.

Not until Cleolin Rao turned her head and looked right at him.

Now, eight months later, in the deep chill of winter, he raised his six-foot-three frame from bed and took two steps to the bathroom. After a while, he would crisscross the bedroom and hall to enter the kitchen and prepare ingredients for the Monday lunchtime cooking ritual he shared with Cleolin.

In his rented place, the kitchen was the largest room. The apartment sat close to his restaurant and his cousin's university. The counters were crowded with spices, bottles of herb-infused oils, and one chipped mug from his first restaurant job in Queens. He filled a pot with water, set it on the stove, and pulled ingredients from the fridge.

Red snapper fillets. Okra. Tomatoes. Scotch bonnet wrapped carefully in plastic. Coconut milk. Thyme.

The menu in his head had a name now: fish stew, city version.

Not the version his grandmother made in Tema, and not the coconut fish curry Cleolin's mother used to cook back in Bengaluru. Something between. Something they had planned for the next meal the nonprofit would serve to their unhoused clients. He would teach volunteers to make it in big pots; she would handle the logistics and paperwork. They had circled the date on a calendar in her kitchen and joked that if the stew flopped, they would blame the weather.

His alarm went off. He silenced it and smiled at the thought of the love of his life, even though she did not know that yet. He would tell her . . . soon.

Kweku cleaned the fish at the sink, his movements efficient. He seasoned the fish, then wrapped it in paper and slid it into a container. Most of the cooking would happen at her place. Her apartment kitchen had become their small, shared country, spiritually somewhere between Ghana and India and Harlem.

He packed up the ingredients, then picked up his black cross-body bag from the chair. The Ghanaian star stitched on the flap had faded at the edges. Inside, he slid his phone, his keys, and a slim black kitchen notebook filled with recipes, notes, and scraps of ideas. A Broadway ticket stub marked his current page.

He paused for a second, thumb resting on the stub.

That play had been their first real date, not just "hanging out after the nonprofit meeting." *Duke and Roya*, the story of an American hip-hop star and an Afghan interpreter in Kabul. He had watched her face more than the stage that night, the way her jaw clenched at certain lines, the way her shoulders dropped when the music swelled.

"I have a weakness for unlikely love stories," she told him afterward on the subway. "They convince me people and love can cross great divides."

He thought of that now and smiled.

"Today," he muttered to himself, "we make something new."

He zipped the bag, shrugged on his jacket, and stepped into the hallway.

His cousin looked up from the couch, where a soccer match was being played on the television.

"You going already?" his cousin asked, voice thick with sleep. That boy was always between sleep, football and food.

"Paradise is waiting," Kweku said. "And if I am late, she will blame me for the rice."

His cousin smirked. "Tell her you face worse heat in the kitchen."

"I will bring her the proof," Kweku replied.

He closed the door and headed down the stairs, the messenger bag snug against his side and the small carrier of food slung on his back.

Paradise

Paradise sat on the edge of Columbia's campus, a modest building that carried itself like something finer. The brass letters of its name were a little dull, and the stone needed cleaning, but once you stepped inside, the lobby still greeted you with a soft kind of pride.

Mahogany panels climbed the walls. Vintage chandeliers washed the marble floor in warm light. A grand piano waited in the corner, still and dusted, a leftover echo of the nights when jazz had filled the room.

Carlos stood at the doorman's desk, dark hair neatly parted, uniform pressed. His posture had become part of the lobby scenery. He knew who skipped rent and who tipped on holidays, who always complained about drafts and who never met his eyes.

At 10:27, he saw the tall Black man hook up his bike to the rails outside the front door and cross the front steps. He had dark-cocoa colored skin, a trimmed beard, and shoulders wide enough to make the glass door look narrow. A food carrier was strapped to his back.

Carlos pressed the buzzer to unlock the door.

"Morning."

"Morning, Carlos, 5F," the man replied.

The way he said Carlos's name always came with a softened "r." His accent set him apart from most of the messengers who rushed through Paradise with Amazon boxes and takeout bags.

Still, routine is a powerful lens. Groceries. Visits. Up and down. Carlos had filed him mentally a few months ago.

Regular delivery guy, except that he knew Carlos' name. Low-key. Polite.

The elevator doors slid open. The man stepped in, turned, and pressed the button. For an instant, he and Carlos made eye contact through the narrowing gap.

Then the doors closed.

Carlos went back to sorting mail.

Love and a Kiss

On the fifth floor, the elevator door opened to a short hallway. The paint on the walls was a little chipped at the corners. A faint smell of someone's incense mixed with the sharper tang of cleaning supplies.

Apartment 5F sat at the end, near a window that looked out on Manhattan Avenue.

Inside, Cleolin hurried between the small living area and the kitchen, tying her long black hair into a loose knot with one hand. She had showered, made filter coffee in the steel *davara* set her aunt sent from Bengaluru, and already answered three work emails for the nonprofit.

The early light caught the warm brown of her skin, a tone that made some people assume she was Latina if she wasn't wearing her bindi or until she opened her mouth and spoke of monsoon rains flooding streets or the particular chaos of home, her accent wrapping around English with the distinctive rhythm of her mother tongue.

Her apartment was a one-bedroom that felt bigger than its measurements. Plants lined the window; a cheap bookshelf leaned against one wall, stuffed with novels and a row of worn Kannada paperbacks from home. Her leather notebook, swollen with clippings and folded flyers, lay on the dining table with a pen tucked sideways into the pages.

In the kitchen nook, rice rested in a saucepan, soaking. She had remembered to rinse it until the water ran almost clear, just like he taught her. A faint scent of cumin drifted up from the pan she had used to temper some spices. The room held traces of both their countries, stitched together by habit and improvisation.

When the knock came, it landed right in the center of her chest, and excitement lit her eyes.

She wiped her hands on a dish towel and opened the door.

Kweku stood there, taller than the frame, NY Mets cap in one hand, a well-worn messenger bag across his chest, the strap of the food carrier overlapping it. His beard outlined the sharpness of his jaw. The burn scar on his forearm was visible where his coat sleeve had pushed back, a smooth, darker patch against his skin.

"You are early," she said.

"You are happy," he answered.

"A little."

"Then I am doing my work," he said, mouth curving.

He stepped inside and set his bag on the counter, the star stitching catching the light. His presence filled the room.

She watched him for a moment, the way his shoulders relaxed when he was here, the way his eyes moved as if mapping the space anew each time.

"You smell like onions," she said.

"I have been faithful to the stew," he replied. "And you smell like coffee."

"Filter coffee," she corrected. "From home. Nothing here tastes the same."

He nodded, then began unpacking ingredients from the carrier and lining them up with a kind of reverence. She handed him a chopping board, and their hands brushed, fingers sliding briefly along skin.

Warmth rose through her at the contact, a slow upward tide.

She busied herself turning on the stove to hide it, trying unsuccessfully to stop herself from grinning.

***

Cooking with Kweku had become its own love language.

He chopped onions with quick, confident motions. She deseeded the scotch bonnet with the caution of someone who had been burned once and learned fast. He told stories about his grandmother tasting stew and wordlessly reaching for more salt without looking, body and memory working together. She talked about her *ajji* in Bengaluru, scooping rice from a battered steel tiffin on Commercial Street, refusing to eat anything that did not smell right.

"When it rained," she said, "we would sit inside and watch the street disappear under water. My brother would try to float bottle caps like boats, and my mother would shout at him to keep his feet out of the drain. The whole world smelled like wet earth and frying chillies."

"I would like to visit there one day," he said, dropping tomatoes into the pan. "Eat something that tastes like your childhood."

"You already are," she answered. "At least on the days you obey instructions."

"I obey sometimes," he said. "When it serves my goals."

"And what are those goals?" she asked, raising one eyebrow.

He looked up from the cutting board, eyes dark and serious now.

"To feed you properly," he said. "To make sure you are not only serving everyone else for the rest of your life."

Oh no, she thought. *This again.*

She swallowed. "I have a job I care about," she reminded him. "The nonprofit needs me. You have seen those files. They would drown in paperwork without me."

"I know," he answered softly. "You are the spine of that place. But you could do more than answer emails and fix schedules. You could lead, Cleo. You could shape what they do."

Cleo. He was the only one here who shortened her name. In his mouth, it sounded like . . . like she was precious. It was more than a nickname.

She turned to the sink to rinse okra, letting the cold water run over her fingers longer than necessary.

"I manage my life just fine," she said. "This apartment. My work. The little I send home to Amma. It is enough."

"You say that," he replied, "but when you talk about the people you serve, your eyes light up. When you talk about forms and budgets, they dim again. You could be the one making decisions that actually change something."

She kept her back toward him.

"That sounds like your dream," she said, voice light. "Not mine."

She was half right. He pictured kitchens, yes. Menus, staff, and the heat of service. But lately, when he imagined a future, it was not just his face in the frame. He saw her in an office above a dining room, papers in one hand, smiling as she looked out over a place they helped create.

"You are right," he said quietly. "I see us doing this together."

He threw his honesty down between them, simple and heavy.

She set the okra down and faced him. His gaze did not waver.

"That is a lot of imagining," she said.

"I have big dreams for us," he replied.

She snorted, but the sound broke and softened at the end.

He reached into his satchel on the counter, pulled out a folded flyer, and smoothed it on the counter with his palm.

"I found this," he said. "A management program at the nonprofit network. They train people who already know community work to run their own centers, their own kitchens. Evening classes. Not far from here."

He pushed the paper toward her.

"Just read it," he said. "You do not have to decide anything today."

She stared at the flyer. The words blurred and reassembled. Tuition covered. Placement support. Sessions on budgeting, staffing, program design.

A familiar resistance rose inside her. Wanting something for herself felt dangerous. Back in Bengaluru, she had watched cousins chase big plans abroad while she stayed behind to help at home. Coming to New York later had felt like using up all her allotted risk.

The idea of reaching again made her ribs feel tight.

"Your stew will burn," she said, reaching for her old defense.

He checked the pot, then glanced back at her, smiling at the deflection.

"You can say no," he said.

"I am not saying anything," she replied.

She looked at the flyer again. He watched her, absentmindedly tapping his thumb on the counter.

"I would apply to something like that myself," he said softly, "but they ask too many questions about history and paperwork. My own situation is not . . ." He trailed off, searching for a word he did not want to use. "Simple," he finished.

They never admitted to his immigration status. The thought of it, shared between them, evaporated.

She folded the flyer once and carried it to the table. Her notebook lay there, spine cracked, stuffed with folded pages and scribbled thoughts. Notes from staff meetings. Ideas for programs she never proposed. Lists of things she would try "if life were different."

She slipped it under a page where she had written, in hurried script, *What if we ran a kitchen?*

The paper stuck out at the edge, stubborn.

"You have an entire book of things you are afraid to want," he said, watching her.

"You are very free with your observations this morning," she replied.

"I have been thinking about this since yesterday. I want you to hear me out."

She rolled her eyes, but a smile tugged at her mouth.

He lifted a spoon toward her.

"Taste," he said.

She stepped close. He held the spoon steady, and she leaned in, lips closing around the stew.

The flavor spilled across her tongue, rich and layered. Smoke, coconut, a clean heat, something that reminded her of both his grandmother's recipe and the fish curries of home. Her eyes closed briefly.

He watched her face with fixed intensity.

"You approve," he asked.

"Don't be smug," she said. "It needs more salt."

He laughed, reached for the salt, and she found herself laughing too.

On impulse, she scooped a piece of fish with her fingers and held it up to his mouth.

"Your turn," she said.

His hand closed lightly around her wrist, and he leaned in, teeth grazing her fingers as he took the bite. His lips brushed her skin. The contact sent a line of heat up her arm.

She did not pull away.

His eyes stayed on hers.

"Now you are the one being dangerous," he said quietly.

"You started it," she answered.

He stepped closer, free hand resting at her waist. The warmth of his palm seeped through the fabric of her shirt.

"You can stop me," he said.

She did not move.

He bent and kissed her.

His mouth met hers with patience and certainty, careful in a way that told her this was not a taking. It was a decision. Their first kiss.

She leaned into him, fingers curling into the fabric of his sleeve, because she had been holding him at the edge of things for months, calling it caution when it was fear. Her aunties would never say his name with ease. They would call her stubborn, impulsive, shameless. An Indian man would have been easier. Familiar. Acceptable. He was none of those things, and she had been bracing for the day love made her choose.

But he had not tried to hurry her into anything she could not stand behind.

He had been showing her, over and over, that he was not a slam-bam-bye man. Not with speeches. With presence. With the way he came when he said he would. With the way he stayed after the work was done. With the way he looked at her like tomorrow mattered.

The stew simmered behind them, pepper and thyme rising warm

into the air, and something sweeter underneath it that made her throat tighten. The part of her that always planned for loss reached for its usual escape, but there was nowhere to put it. Not with his hand at her waist, steady, not asking, not taking.

A word rose in her, uninvited and absolute.

Mine.

When they parted, she caught her breath in a small, soundless gasp.

"This is a bad idea," she said, voice low.

"Why?" he asked.

"Because I will like it," she admitted. "And then you could leave."

His hand tightened once at her waist, not possessive, just firm, as if he needed her to understand.

"I'm here," he said. "I'm not going anywhere."

Somewhere deep in the old, listening place his grandmother used to call the ground of truth, something skipped a beat. *Promises like that,* she always said, *made spirits lift their heads.*

Kweku kissed Cleolin's forehead and stepped back.

"Rice," he said. "Before it turns to paste."

She let out a breath and forced herself to turn back to the stove. He busied himself with plates and bowls, but a small part of him felt oddly watched, as if unseen elders had turned their heads at his words.

He shook off the feeling. There was work to do, a life to build, a stew to perfect.

The Accident

They ate at her small table by the window that overlooked Manhattan Avenue. Traffic moved below, a slow river of cars and buses. The sky was a clear, hard blue.

They talked about the nonprofit, about his cousin's late-night soccer obsession, about the smell of first rain in granite city streets.

At one point, she glanced at his forearm.

"How did you get that scar?" she asked.

He looked down.

"A grill line in Astoria," he said. "One of the new cooks panicked when the flame flared. I grabbed the pan and pulled him back. The oil did not care which arm it kissed. It chose mine."

She winced. "That must have hurt."

"It did," he said. "But he stayed in the kitchen because of it. He is a sous chef now. Worth the price."

She shook her head. "You are always throwing yourself between people and heat."

"Maybe," he said. "Maybe that is what I am for."

She thought of her own life, standing between her clients and the worst of the systems that pushed them onto the street. Between landlords and tenants who could not read the fine print. Between her mother and the news that would only worry her.

"We are both shields," she said.

"Then we should learn to shield each other, too," he replied.

What she heard beneath his words was simple: *we can carry this together. No one is stronger here.* She had not known he felt that from the first day, though something in her had sensed it. And now, sitting in front of him, she felt safe in a way that calmed her.

After they finished eating, he stood and began to clear the table.

"I owe my aunt thyme," he said. "If I do not bring it today, she will tell the whole family I neglected her cooking."

"You and your aunt are very serious about herbs," she said.

"Her *suya* will humble your entire building," he replied. "I stay on her good side."

He pulled his hat from the back of a chair and slung his bag over his shoulder.

"I will be back in fifteen minutes," he said. "Twenty, if the line is long."

"Do not hurry," she said. "I have dishes to do and a flyer to pretend I am not reading."

"You will read it," he said confidently.

"We will see," she answered.

At the door, he hesitated, then cupped her face with one hand and kissed her again, softer but no less firm.

"I like you in this light," he said.

"Which light?" she asked.

"This one," he replied. "Where you are almost ready to admit you want something."

She shoved his shoulder lightly.

"Go and buy your thyme," she said. "Before your aunt disowns you."

"Yes, miss," he said, grinning.

He left, the door clicking shut behind him.

She stood there staring at the wood for a moment, then shook herself and turned back to the kitchen. The bowls went into the sink. The pot soaked. She stacked plates with the efficiency of someone who had learned to keep busy when her heart started trying to run ahead of her head.

She wiped down the counter, poured herself more coffee, and finally gave in. The calfskin planner waited on the table. She opened it, slid the flyer fully into view, and began to read.

She did not glance at the clock. She did not listen for sirens any more than she usually did. He was buying herbs a few blocks away. There was no reason in the world to assume anything else.

***

The accident happened near the light at the corner.

Kweku rode with his hood up, cap visor low on his forehead, bag hugging his body. The street was busy but not more dangerous than usual. Taxi horns. A delivery truck double-parked. A woman dragging a suitcase over a patch of ice.

He waited for the walk sign, then pushed off, bike gliding into the crosswalk.

He did not see the car until it was almost on top of him. Later, witnesses would explain that the driver had tried to beat the light. That the sun hit the windshield at a bad angle. That everyone moved a little too fast.

Impact knocked the breath from him before he could curse.

He flew sideways. Time stretched into a razor-thin thread.

The cold slap of air.

The instant recognition that this could be the thing that changed everything or ended it.

Then the ground.

He hit hard and the world contracted to a single blast of pain that ran the length of his body.

His bag strap snapped, dangled loose and skidded across the asphalt, spilling its contents. His iPhone cracked against the curb, spiderwebs blooming across the glass. Keys scattered, shining briefly in the winter sun before sliding to a stop near a storm drain.

The sounds of Harlem rushed back in, someone shouting, brakes squealing, a chorus of "Oh my God" from the sidewalk.

He blinked.

For a strange moment, the brightness around him seemed to separate from the sky. A line of figures stood just beyond the ring of onlookers. Old faces and young ones, familiar and not. Cloth patterns his grandmother had sewn, hats his grandfather used to wear, a boyhood cousin who had died of fever when they were both ten.

They did not speak, but he felt their intention clearly, the way he felt the pull of hot oil when it was about to burn.

Come, their presence said. *We are here.*

Not a command. A calling.

He thought of Cleolin up on five, her hands in soap suds. Later, brow furrowed over a flyer she pretended not to want. He thought of the stew in her pot, the smell of coconut in that small kitchen, the feel of her fingers against his mouth as she fed him.

"I just told her I am not going anywhere," he tried to say.

What came out was a soft, wet breath.

A man knelt at his side, face pale, hands hovering.

"Stay with us," the stranger urged. "Ambulance is coming. Breathe!"

The figures at the edge of his vision did not move closer, nor did they recede. They waited, patient. The world around him blurred at the edges.

He did not hear the siren arrive so much as feel the sound buzzing through the ground into his bones.

Hands pressed at his neck. Questions floated above him, directed at one another, not at him.

Then something inside let go.

The pain dropped away. The cold air warmed. The sky opened in a way that had nothing to do with weather.

The figures turned, and he understood where Asamando lay. Not in the clouds, not under the earth, but in a place that held all of them at once, his people and their people, folded into one long, living story.

He followed.

***

Carlos did not see the exact moment the car struck.

The noise hit first, a sharp slam of metal and a woman's shout. From the lobby door of Paradise, Carlos saw people twisting toward the intersection, shoulders tightening, a small crowd beginning to form. Something lay in the street, but bodies hid most of the view.

He stepped outside, the cold hitting his face as he moved down the short path to the sidewalk. The closer he got, the clearer the scene became. A bike sprawled near the crosswalk, frame twisted. A black sling bag lay half open on the pavement, the Ghanaian star on its flap scuffed. A cracked phone glinted by the curb. Keys rested near the drain.

Then he saw the man at the center of it all, on the cold road, surrounded by strangers trying to help.

For a second, Carlos did not place the face. Without the usual easy stride and the bag across his chest, the man looked smaller. Younger.

He moved closer, stopping just outside the ring of people.

Paramedics were already kneeling beside the cyclist, hands moving with knowledgeable quickness.

"Male, thirties," one said. "Head trauma, possible spinal."

They lifted the body onto a stretcher with a coordination that seemed almost gentle. Carlos caught a glimpse of the man's face. Eyes closed. Jaw slack. A smear of blood at the hairline.

He had watched this man press elevator buttons and nod hello for months. He had never stopped him to say more than "good morning."

Now strangers strapped him down and loaded him into the ambulance.

The doors closed. The siren rose, then pulled away into traffic. The small body of people quickly dispersed into their respective daily lives.

Carlos stayed rooted to the spot until the sound faded.

Then he walked back to where the messenger-type bag had landed. Someone had pushed it onto the sidewalk. The strap was torn clean through. For some reason he could not explain, Carlos picked it up and carried it back to Paradise.

His colleague stood at the lobby desk.

"Where were you, man?"

Carlos remained mute. Having just borne witness to death, watching someone slip away from this world. he set the messenger bag gently onto one shelf in the doorman's cabinet. Then he retrieved his lunch bag and continued without a word to the enclave behind the lobby. In the staff lounge, he pulled out his corned beef Pandesal sandwich and contemplated the life cut short, and what it might mean to him.

What are you doing with your own time, Carlos?

***

Upstairs, Cleolin finished washing the dishes and poured herself another cup of coffee. The filter hissed as the last of the water dripped through. She took a sip, grimaced; it had gone a little bitter while she was distracted.

She opened her notebook and made a list of tasks for the afternoon. A grant report. A phone call with a social worker about a client who needed a bed before the weekend. A spreadsheet that would not build itself.

Every now and then, the smell of the stew lingered in the corners of the room, warm and comforting and sharp. She smiled without meaning to, thinking of the way he had said, *I see us doing this together.*

She did not check the clock. She trusted his fifteen minutes would be more like twenty-five like they always did, but not enough to worry her.

When her phone rang, it startled her only because she was deep in a sentence.

Unknown number.

"Hello," she said.

"Is this Ms. Cleolin Rao?" a voice asked. The speaker's tone was careful, professional.

"Yes," she said slowly.

"I am calling from Harlem Hospital," the woman said. "Is this a good time to talk?"

The question tilted something inside her.

"Yes," she answered, though her palms had begun to sweat.

"A man named Kweku Mensah was brought in from a street collision near your building," the woman continued. "We found your number written in his notebook contacts, listed under 'Fiancée.' I am very sorry, but he died from his injuries a short time ago. We tried to resuscitate him, but it was not possible."

The room stayed exactly where it was, but her knees softened. She reached blindly for the back of a chair and held on to herself.

"Fiancée," she repeated, but very quietly.

"I know this is a shock," the woman said. "We need someone who knew him to come by and collect his personal belongings. There is also paperwork we will ask a family member to complete. Do you know how to reach any relatives?"

Her mind scrambled for footing. Aunt. Cousin. The stories he told. Loud, boisterous Sunday family dinners in Queens. She saw his aunt's face in flashes from photos he shared.

"Yes," she said. "He has an aunt in Queens. I can come in today."

The woman gave directions and a case number. When the call ended, the silence in the apartment changed texture.

The stew pot on the stove looked obscene. The bowls in the drying rack glinted with a brightness that hurt her eyes.

She drew a breath that did not seem to fill her lungs and forced herself to move.

She moved mechanically, pulling on jeans, a sweater, and her heavy coat, before grabbing her scarf, boots, purse, and cross-body bag.

She locked the door to 5F, hand trembling only once, and went to meet the version of him who, she would learn, now only existed on forms and charts and tags.

The News

At the hospital, fluorescent light flattened everything. The nurse at the desk recognized her name and handed over a clear plastic bag.

Inside were the clothes he was wearing, his cracked phone, wallet, recipe notebook, and keys, along with the chipped Tottenham keychain.

"Where is his leather cross-body bag?"

"These were the only items that came here with him," the nurse said gently. "Everything else must have been lost at the scene."

Cleolin stared at the plastic package, her throat too tight to speak. It looked nothing like a life. It barely looked like a person. *He wanted to marry me?*

The nurse said gently. "I am very sorry for your loss."

Cleolin's mind continued to spiral around, *fianceé.* "We were . . ." She stopped, throat tightening. Words would not line up properly. "We did not talk about that yet."

The nurse nodded, not knowing what the woman was referring to but knowing she had seen many kinds of not-yets.

"There is a social worker who will coordinate with his family for the rest," the nurse said. "You do not have to carry that alone."

The nurse nodded and stepped away.

In a shadowed part of the corridor, Cleolin opened the bag and fished around irritably.

She felt his wallet in his jacket pocket. It was worn soft at the edges. Inside, she found a MetroCard, a handful of receipts folded into neat squares, and a small piece of paper tucked behind his ID. Numbers written in tidy handwriting. Nothing labeled.

She stared at it for a long time before reaching for his phone.

The screen lit up.

She entered the first set of numbers on his list.

The device unlocked.

Not fate. Not romance. Just something practical he left for himself in case he forgot. That steadiness felt like him.

Her breath stopped.

There was his wallpaper: a photo he had taken of the stew they made last month, her hand blurred in the corner as she reached in to taste it. App icons. A missed call from his aunt. A text thread with her own name at the top.

She swallowed hard and tapped to pull up his contacts. His aunt's number sat under "Auntie Ama."

Her thumb hovered over the call button.

Inexplicably, Cleolin wondered at that moment of life after death. She remembered the stories he told about his ancestors visiting in dreams. She thought of her own grandparents, long gone, whose presence she sometimes felt in the way the light hit her kitchen tile.

Tears pricked her eyes sharply. She shook her head and tapped.

The call connected on the second ring.

When she said his name, Auntie Ama already knew. Or maybe she understood the moment a stranger's voice spoke from his phone. The older woman's cry came through the line raw and immediate, as if the grief had been waiting just behind her breath.

"I am so sorry," Cleolin managed. "There was an accident. I have his phone. I wanted to reach someone."

Auntie Ama thanked her in broken phrases, voice trembling. They exchanged only what was needed. No details. No plans. Just the confirmation that he would not come back.

"I will call when . . . when we know more," the aunt whispered.

"Yes," Cleolin said. "Of course."

When she hung up, her legs felt heavy, as if someone had tied whole days to her ankles.

Going Home

A week passed before the next call came.

Kweku's cousin introduced himself softly, saying Auntie Ama had asked him to reach out now that the family had gathered and plans were set.

"We are holding his going-home ceremony this weekend," he said. "We would like you to come, if you want. My aunt says he spoke of you often."

"I'll be there," she said.

"Good," the cousin replied. "He would like that."

***

She called in sick to the nonprofit for a second week. Her supervisor's voice on the phone mixed sympathy with barely concealed panic about reports and meetings. Cleolin sent a short, firm email afterward: I will be offline for several days. Please redistribute the workload.

She spent hours in her apartment, sitting on the floor by the window, staring at Manhattan Avenue below. The city never stopped. People crossed at the same corner where he fell, heads down, bags in hand. Buses pulled up, swallowed bodies, emptied out again.

In the in-between moments, grief came in waves that left her gasping. Not just for the man he had been, but for the future that had begun to collect around them like steam. Thursday dinners. Volunteers learning his recipes. A program he pushed her toward, where for once she might be building something instead of just maintaining it.

One afternoon, she opened his recipe notebook. The cover was worn. Grease stains marked the edges. Inside, his handwriting curled across pages in blue ink.

The Broadway ticket stub marked one section. She slid it aside and smiled despite herself when she saw the title.

Fish stew, city version.

Notes lined the margins. *Adjust for shelter kitchen. Bigger pots. Less pepper for newcomers, more on the side. Ask Cleo about vegetarian option.*

Her eyes blurred.

***

The ceremony that weekend drew her to a church basement in Queens where his family had set up tables and a framed photo of him. Fluorescent lights buzzed overhead, casting a flat glow on the crowd gathered around foil trays of food and plastic pitchers of ginger drink.

Cleolin arrived in a simple black dress that fell just below her knees, the one she wore to work meetings when she needed to look unruffled even if she did not feel it. Her long black hair was pulled into a low braid that brushed her collarbone. Her light-brown skin looked almost golden under the harsh basement lighting, making her feel even more exposed among strangers who shared his deeper cocoa tone.

Auntie Ama met her at the door, shoulders squared, chin set. She pulled Cleolin into a tight, brief embrace and stepped back just as quickly.

"You are the one from Paradise. He talked about you."

Cleolin processed this quietly. Kweku had never given any indication that he wanted her to meet his family.

"You came. Good," the older woman said. Her tone carried authority, not warmth, but her hand stayed on Cleolin's arm a moment too long. "Sit. Eat something. Your face is empty."

"He talked about all of you," Cleolin said finally.

She sat in a folding chair among rows of people whose faces held pieces of him. Men with the same strong jaw. Women with the same determined eyes. Children whose laughter rang like the stories he told her about his cousins.

Her dress, her accent, her lighter skin, her hesitant grasp of Twi, all of it marked her as different. She felt like a guest at a family reunion and a trespasser in someone else's grief at the same time.

The cousin who had called swooped in even as she was sorting through this feeling, his words spilling in a rush.

"Sorry about the late notice of the arrangements, Cleo. Auntie did not make a note of your number so we had to go through her phone and call back every incoming call. As you can imagine, there were so many calls that day. Finally, Eva, that is Kweku's sister, well, not his biological sister, she is a close tribe member, close in age, so we call her our sister. Anyway, Eva said we were stupid and said that yours would have been the first call, but that was not true because Auntie has so many people calling her . . ."

Cleolin blinked, trying to keep up.

The cousin pressed a glass of water into her hand. "Drink. You must be exhausted. Are you okay? I mean, not okay-okay but . . . you know."

His nervous laugh bubbled out.

Then he blinked, and tears filled his eyes. Cleolin was horrified that this reaction came from her presence alone.

The one who must be Eva stepped forward, eyes red and swollen.

She tapped the cousin on the shoulder and he choked on a sob and rushed away.

"I am sorry, I did not mean . . ." Cleolin stopped when Eva wrapped her arms around her and held on.

When she finally let go, her voice shook. "He talked about you. All the time. I am sorry. I am so sorry."

Her apology broke into another quiet sob.

They sang. They prayed. They told stories about him. Some were small, like how he always made the tea too strong. Some were large, like the night he stayed late to cook for a shelter after a snowstorm even though his shift had ended hours earlier.

His cousin caught her eye at one point and lifted a hand in recognition. She lifted hers back, the gesture small but anchoring.

Later, another sister approached her. Younger, with his eyes, wearing a simple black dress and a scarf tied loosely over her hair.

"You are Cleo," she said.

"Yes," Cleolin answered.

"He had your photo saved," the sister said.

Emotion rose in Cleolin's throat. "I am sorry," she managed. "For all of this."

"We are sorry with you," the sister replied.

The phrasing caught her. The inclusion and distance. Both true. She tried to seem serene inside the storms of all this grief for Kweku.

On the train back to Harlem, she stared at her reflection in the darkened window, her braid resting tiredly on her shoulder, her dress creased from sitting too long. She did not recognize the expression on her face. Grief and something like resolve had begun to knit themselves into a new shape.

The Recipe

Today was the hundredth day since Kweku died.

Cleolin stood in her kitchen with his notebook open on the counter.

Fish stew, city version.

She rolled up her sleeves and set rice to soak. She cleaned fish over the sink, fingers moving more slowly than his ever had. She chopped onions until her eyes stung, and she could not tell if it was the knife or the memory.

Thyme crackled in the pan. Coconut milk thickened the broth. She dropped in a full scotch bonnet instead of the cautious half she would typically use. Her body wanted the fire, something she could feel instead of swallow.

The smell rose again, familiar and devastating. Pepper and smoke and the soft sweetness of coconut curled through the room. She turned and stepped over to her window overlooking Manhattan Avenue.

Down below, the corner where he had fallen looked almost ordinary. A kid in a red jacket waited to cross. A woman with a stroller hurried past. A delivery cyclist paused at the light, foot braced on the curb, eyes on the signal.

She pressed her palm against the glass for a moment, then went back to the stove.

When the stew finished, she ladled a full portion into the same bowl he had used that morning he died. The ceramic warmed her palms.

She covered the bowl with foil, took a breath, and pulled on her coat.

This time, she did not feel like running from the corner. She felt pulled toward it.

***

She stood where the accident happened, the container of stew warm in her hands. Traffic hissed by, obnoxious and indifferent. A man in a thick, grimy coat lingered near the bus stop, rubbing his palms together for warmth—pale skin chapped raw, a shopping cart of possessions nearby.

"It's fucking May," he cursed at the freakish snow falling around them, at winter's grip refusing to let go of New York.

She cleared her throat. "Sir? Would you like some food? I made too much."

He looked at the container, not at her, assessing it with the practiced eye of someone who had taken meals wherever he could find them.

"You cooked it?" he asked.

"Yes," she said.

He accepted it with both hands. "Appreciate it." He lifted the lid and inhaled. "Smells good. Real good."

For a moment, that was all. No sudden recognition. No wise pronouncements. Just a man grateful for a hot meal on a cold day.

He gave her a small nod. "Bless you," he added, then turned toward a bench and began to eat with single-minded focus.

Cleolin watched him for a few seconds longer than she meant to. Something in the ease of his posture, the simple acceptance of the food, steadied her spirit. She wasn't sure why, but offering it felt right.

As she walked away, she held the emptiness inside her like a fragile bowl, warmed briefly by the way he had eaten without asking for the story behind it.

Mysteriously, in her head, she heard the lines of a song Kweku had been singing since he visited her in her building. *It's just another day, for you and me, in Paradise.*

"I hate that you died!" She breathed out an angry whisper to the man who only lived in her head and heart.

***

As Cleolin entered Paradise, her own thoughts held her captive. Images of Kweku kept flashing across her mind, mixed with the face of the homeless man on the corner. She moved through the warm lobby on autopilot.

"I am sorry to bother you," a voice said in a gentle tone.

She startled.

Carlos stood near the doorman's desk in full uniform, cap tucked under his arm. He held a black sling bag with both hands. The torn strap dangled like a loose thread.

She blinked, fresh shock rising through her whole body.

"I think this is his," he said.

The Ghanaian star on the flap gleamed under the lobby lights. She reached out, fingers clutching the canvas as if it might vanish.

"I picked it up from the street that morning," Carlos said. His voice stayed steady, but his eyes drifted past her, toward the glass doors. "Right outside. Near Paradise." He cleared his throat. "I kept meaning to bring it down."

She nodded, unable to speak.

He hesitated, then added, almost to himself, "I was cutting a pomegranate earlier. In the back." A small, uncertain shake of his head. "The seeds bursting out, juice dripping. . . it made me think of him." He looked at the bag again. ". . . and I remembered I still had this bag. I did not know about you and him . . ."

"You did not have to . . ." Her voice came out thin, but the lift of her chin carried her thanks.

Carlos nodded. "He always gave me the time of day. Most people don't. But you . . .. and him . . ."

She pulled the bag to her chest. The weight felt strange. It was lighter than it should have been.

Carlos took her in. Her hair was pulled back any which way, dark circles settled under her eyes, lips dry and cracked. The hoodie she wore carried the faint sour smell of long hours and missed sleep. She looked nothing like she had before Kweku died.

"You all right, miss?" he asked.

She swallowed. "I'm fine."

He stepped back, giving her space. "If you ever need anything, I'm here most days."

"Thank you," she said, managing a tight smile.

She walked toward the elevators with slow, uneven steps. The bag that she pressed to her chest created a sensation of being held while also intensifying her loneliness. Inside her apartment, she locked the door and slid down to the floor. The room held nothing but her breath.

Only then did she unzip the bag.

Her hand searched.

Nothing.

No notebook. No keys. No scraps of paper.

No trace of the life he carried with him everywhere.

An empty shell.

She rested the bag on her knees and closed her eyes, letting out a long, weary breath..

The Future

Cleolin woke before the sun reached her windows. She lay still on the couch, knees tucked under the thin blanket she had pulled over herself hours earlier, having never made it to her bedroom. The apartment was quiet.

On the coffee table sat Kweku's things she never returned to his family: his football team keychain, his phone, his hoodie. She stared at them, then slid her hand out from beneath the blanket and picked up the keychain.

She had turned it over in her palm so many times in the past three months that some of the enamel had rubbed to dull metal. Once, it had carried his whole presence with it. *Come on you Spurs!* he would say!

Come on you, she mouthed.

She should have given these things to Auntie. Ninety-nine days ago. But every time she imagined handing them over, a terror gripped her body, as if something essential would disappear along with his things.

She set the keychain down and exhaled.

The stew pot she used last night sat on the drying rack, turned upside down, clean and silent. Cooking for the man on the corner had felt like a pulse of her old self.

She wasn't ready to say it out loud yet, but her whole spirit was aching for change. She was ready to be less sad, but felt guilty about it.

She drew her knees tighter under the blanket and whispered into the quiet, "I need something new, Kweku."

With her next exhale, she sat up and stretched.

"Ahhhhhhhhhh."

She opened her laptop. The screen lit up. She navigated to the site. A simple form. A few questions she could answer in minutes. But her hands hovered above the keyboard without touching a single key.

The cursor blinked in the first field.

Name.

"Cleolin," she whispered it aloud, as if testing whether the sound made her feel steadier. It didn't.

Cleolin closed the laptop and set it aside.

She splayed her hands on her lap, and for the first time in weeks, she paid attention to her fingers. The half-moons under her nails were dark with old grit she hadn't bothered to scrub out. Her cuticles were dry and uneven. She used to fuss obsessively over her hands, but somewhere along the way grief had taken that from her too.

She let out a shaky breath. The urge to push herself into a grand transformation evaporated. She didn't have the capacity for that. Not today.

She stood, walked to the bathroom, and turned on the tap. Warm water filled the sink. She soaked her fingers, worked the dirt out slowly, trimmed what needed trimming, and let the smallness of the task comfort her. This she could manage. This she could control.

I'm not ready for management training, Kweku. She was barely ready to keep breathing. But maybe she would try again tomorrow. Or the day after.

One step. Then another. Nothing more than that.

***

She made it to her bedroom that night, but she could not sleep. So, she scrolled through her phone. Her social media notifications were overflowing, but one tag from the nonprofit caught her eye.

A volunteer had posted a photo of Kweku's cooking station from the last outreach event. Stainless steel trays, a row of ladles, his handwriting taped to the wall with instructions for the spice mix.

Rest easy, brother. You cooked like you meant it. Thank you for feeding us all.

Below it, a thread had formed. Dozens of comments.

A shelter staff member wrote, "He showed up during the snowstorm when no one else could get across town. He cooked for forty people without asking for anything in return."

A woman replied, "I only talked to him twice, but he remembered my child's name the second time. People like that are rare."

Someone from his old restaurant in Astoria added a photo of him on a busy night, sweat on his forehead, smiling anyway.

"He trained half our kitchen. Always patient. Always lifting someone else up."

Then she saw a short video posted by his cousin in Ghana. Just ten seconds.

Kweku at a family gathering, laughing with a plate balanced in one hand and a toddler on his hip. In the caption his cousin wrote, *He carried our joy like it was light.*

Cleolin watched the video more times than she meant to. In the soft glow of her phone, she saw versions of him he had never shown her. A whole community speaking his name with tenderness.

For the first time since the funeral, she felt the grief shift. Not smaller. Not easier. But shared.

She placed the phone facedown on the bed. The room felt different. Not less empty, but less lonely.

Wide awake now, she sat up straighter in bed after propping up the pillows. She reached for her laptop.

She clicked on the application link and watched the form load slowly across the screen.

Her name belonged in the first field. That was simple enough. She typed the first letter, then stopped. Her stomach tightened. Something about typing her own name felt like a promise she was not sure she could keep.

She closed the laptop halfway. Then opened it again. She pushed herself up from the bed, dragging the blanket with her, and walked into the living room. The small desk in the corner waited in its usual silence, papers stacked neatly beside the monitor. She sat, pulled the chair close, and set the laptop down as if placing something fragile.

All right, she told herself. One line. Just one.

She typed her full name and pressed enter before she lost her nerve. The next question asked for a brief statement of interest. Her fingers hovered over the keys. The words she might have written when he was alive caught in her throat now.

Why here? What do you hope to build?

She whispered, "I do not know." Hearing the uncertainty aloud hurt more than she expected.

She tried again, writing three sentences only to delete two, rewrite one, and eventually delete that one as well. With her pulse thudding in her ears, she pushed the chair back and stood, breathing hard like she had run somewhere.

She paced the length of her living room. Twice. Three times.

Then she returned to the table and sat down.

She typed a single honest line.

"I want to learn how to help people without disappearing in the process."

She read it twice. She did not know if it was the right answer, or if she had anything left to give. But she kept going, one field at a time.

By the time she reached the final page, her hands were trembling.

She hovered over the submit button. Her breath faltered.

"I am not ready," she whispered.

The screen waited.

She looked toward the bathroom door and pictured Kweku leaning there, eyebrows raised, asking with his eyes, *What do you want?*

"I want more," she said. The words felt heavy and grinding, like putting a stone in the ground and claiming the space around it.

More than grief. More than holding everything together in the background. More joy. More life.

"But I am afraid, Kweku," she said to him who had become her guardian in the way of the Akan.

She imagined him smiling at that. Not dismissing the fear, just nodding as if to say, *You can still move. Press submit anyway.*

So she did.

The confirmation page loaded. No rush of relief. No triumph. Just a quiet recognition that she had crossed a line she could not uncross.

This was not closure. It was the first hard step on a road she never planned to travel.

She closed the laptop and rested both hands on its cover until the shaking eased.

She was still afraid.

He did not come back, but the life he pointed her toward had begun its slow arrival.

And she would meet it.

181

All the Versions of Love

Fragment I (Day 0)

It was a Friday night, almost a year ago, when my wife first told me she was married to my best friend.

That evening, we had gone to see a dreadful and disappointing play at the local theatre. Then we had a scrumptious dinner at an overpriced Italian restaurant next to the playhouse, before stopping into the corner shop downstairs from our apartment to pick up 'essentials' to close out our date night.

I went for the cheese; she went for the wine.

"Wow," I whispered when I saw the shop had Oscypek cheese. The attendant stocking next to me looked up and said, "You like that cheese?"

"Yes, I remember it from my country." I turned it over in my hand, almost reverently.

"We've carried it for a long time. It's a favorite in the neighborhood. I place it front and center. It definitely has its fans; folks come to our little shop for it specifically."

I looked down at him. I've always towered over most people; even now, at fifty-two, my shoulders still square out the way they did in my college basketball days, though my belly has long since surrendered to late-night takeout and deadline stress. "Really? I've never seen it here."

Laying the cheese in the shopping basket, I strode to the wine section, counting the dead bulbs as I passed. One. Two. My strange habit made me notice that the lighting in the shop was off this evening. Three. Four. My knees cracked a little as I stepped over a crate the stock boy had left in the aisle. I'd stopped pretending that was a fresh development; bodies announce their fifties whether you admit it or not.

Then, I felt something was off with her, too. My wife was standing, her back to me, her fingers skimming over the neck of a bottle. She was humming under her breath. Oddly, it was three notes of what should have been a familiar hymn, but she hummed it off-key. Her thumb kept circling the label.

"Georgieta?"

She turned around when she heard her name. She looked . . . surprised.

Why? I wonder.

"Jakub," she said my name strangely and asked, "You remember me?"

At that moment, my experience as a consultant helped me. Over the years, I had heard many wildly surprising views, ignorant assumptions, and other naïve conclusions from my clients. I had learned to be professional, emotionally intelligent, and thoughtful in my responses without making the purveyor of the insane ideas seem crazy.

I never had to do this in my marriage until now.

With a poker face, I looked my tall, beautiful wife directly in her eyes as my mind slid through the many explanations of what was happening to us at this moment.

She's role-playing! This was the only logical answer, I concluded. She was trying to get us to put on a better performance than the one we saw earlier that evening. Okay, I will play along, my love.

"I remember you," I said, nodding, as I scrutinized her dark, honey-smooth face for signs of delight that I figured out her game. Her thick dreadlocks were unpinned tonight, coily and soft against her neck, catching the aisle's bad light like threads of ink.

"You were a powerful consultant at one of the Big 4 firms. One of a few Black people and the only person from a country in Africa."

I pulled this tidbit out of our reality. We met at a conference more than two decades ago. She was on a panel of experts, and her face, body, and voice all arrested my attention in a way that shocked me. I had never seen someone like her in these circles before. She stood out.

I remember leaning over to the man on my right. Nuru. He was my college roommate, best friend, and business partner.

"Nuru, do you know her?"

"I know I always give you a hard time for assuming all Africans know each other," he said with that velvet warmth that could sand the edge off any room, "but I actually do know her. Georgieta Koroma. She's from my country. Our families know each other well."

"She's from Ghana? Brother, I need to meet her."

Nuru did not respond then; before her panel finished, he vanished. I did not wait for him. I found her and pursued her. For the next five months, I made it my mission to be everything she desired. Later, with a dazzling and toothy smile, she said, "Yes!", fulfilling my desire to marry her. We've been together ever since.

But now, at this moment, twenty-five years later, I released our history to pretend we were strangers and said, "I didn't think I'd ever see you again."

"Life happens, doesn't it?" she said. "You should know, I was married once."

"What?"

"I was married to Nuru."

Stunned, I blinked. I reflexively swallowed before realizing my throat was dry.

"Nuru . . . my best friend? You were married to Nuru Mensah?"

Above us, the fluorescent light blinked on, and a harsh glare fell on us. I looked up, eyebrows knotted, mind racing again. What kind of disgusting game was this?

"Yes. Do you know him?" she asked, as what seemed like worry and sadness tightened the muscles on her face.

I stayed silent. Tension, worry, and anger coiled within me. Had my wife been married before we exchanged vows, and I did not know? Married to my best friend, who said nothing! Was I duped? *Co kurwa!* Polish obscenities would pour out in an unrelenting stream if I dared open my mouth. Certain of that, I pressed my lips together in a thin line. My face flushed.

"I'm sorry to say, he died," she said.

"What?"

"Nuru. He died of prostate cancer, er . . ." Her eyes looked at the floor, then at the shelves. She shook her head and closed her eyes tight. "Um . . . I . . . I can't remember exactly when."

I relaxed then. Something was wrong. My wife would never feign marriage to someone else, and she would never pretend that my best friend, our friend, was dead, knowing that he was very much alive.

"It's okay, Georgieta. Let me take you home."

She blinked, her eyes darting to the Oscypek cheese still in my basket. "You like that one?" she said softly, the same way she always did when we picnicked. Her tone steadied something between us, and I watched the tension in her shoulders ease. I could tell she didn't know why she trusted me, only that she did. When I held out my hand, she took it, hesitant but willing.

Fragment II (Day 5)

The following Wednesday, I explained the situation to the primary care physician.

"Doctor, we've been noticing some changes," I said. "Georgieta's been getting confused."

Since the other night, I felt the weight of the lie I'd been telling myself was years in the making. It wasn't just the play at the local theatre. It was probably hundreds of small things I'd trained myself not to notice.

"I understand your concern, Jakub," the doctor said, leaning forward. "And Georgieta, thank you for coming in. Can you tell me what you've been experiencing?"

Georgieta smiled, uncertain, and looked at me. She paused, then began. "Jakub says I . . . sometimes words slip away. And memories. I think."

"It's more than that, Doctor," I said.

Georgieta pressed her lips together and shifted in her chair, angling her body away from mine.

I knew my honesty might feel like a betrayal, but the turn her story took the other night scared me to death. I had to know if what she was saying now was fact or fiction.

"It's been happening for years," I said. "The off-key melodies she repeats under her breath. The afternoon she couldn't find the road to the market, three summers ago. I treated each moment like a faulty light, something I could ignore until it corrected itself. I told myself she was just tired. Then recently, it shifted from forgetting to remembering things that were entirely wrong."

The doctor nodded. "It's rarely a sudden change, Jakub. These things often begin quietly, long before they're named. The mind fills in the gaps for as long as it can."

Georgieta's smile faltered. Confusion crossed her face, sharp and unguarded. "You're being dramatic, Jakub!" she said. "Three years ago? I was fine." She turned to the doctor, her voice firming. "He's always exaggerated my little quirks."

"I see," the doctor said, her gaze moving between us. "We'll run some tests. And I'd like to refer you to a neurologist for a more thorough evaluation."

Fragment III (Day 13)

The specialist, Dr. Li Na Chen, explained, "The neuroimaging shows some . . . abnormalities. We need to consider the possibility of early cognitive decline."

Her white coat was plain, sleeves pushed to the wrist, ruby studs at her ears. She opened a palm-sized notebook bristling with colored tabs, tapped her pen once, then stilled it. I presumed this was a habit.

"Cognitive decline? What does that mean?"

Dr. Chen looked at me, then turned to Georgieta and smiled, then spoke in a comforting tone. "It means there's a change in your brain function, affecting memory, thinking, and language."

"*Ɛnyɛ hwee*," Georgieta murmured under her breath, then frowned. Did she still know what these Ghanaian words meant? Her fingers worried the seam of her skirt as if she could pull the right thought from the fabric.

Dr. Chen didn't flinch at the foreign language; she simply nodded and said, "We'll need more tests to determine the extent of the decline and whether it's young onset." A tiny rubber brain sat beside her monitor; she didn't squeeze it, only rested two fingers there, a metronome for her tone.

Georgieta's smile didn't reach her eyes. "I used to remember everyone's name on a project," she said faintly. "Now I lose words mid-sentence." Her voice cracked a little. "Will I forget him, too?" she asked, not looking at me.

No one spoke for four uncomfortable seconds.

I gave a nervous chuckle and said, "You keep this room cold on purpose, don't you? To keep us from panicking?"

Dr. Chen didn't bite. "To keep the machines from overheating," she said, her smile tight but kind.

Dr. Chen flipped to a blue-tabbed page when we were alone. "Blue is for home protocols," she said softly. "Watch her body language. Match her reality. Don't contradict or correct; it only causes distress. Let her lead the conversation. Look for patterns in her new memories. They might tell us something important or be proxies for actual events or people."

I remembered this when Georgieta woke up in the middle of the night two days later. She looked at me, and I knew. I had quickly become adept at reading the signs. Withdrawn, her gaze distant, she seemed lost in another world.

Carefully, I opened my arms. "I'm here, my love. I'm here."

"Jakub?" She says my name like a question, like we're meeting for the first time in years. "I didn't expect to see you here."

I slip into the role she's cast me in. "It's been a while," I say, careful to keep my tone neutral, friendly but not too familiar.

"It has," she agrees, then hesitates. "I . . . I'm married now. Was married. To Nuru."

Shit, this again! My heart clenches, but I keep my face composed. This is the hardest part: hearing her speak of Nuru, my oldest friend, as her lost love.

I no longer considered our marriage in terms of the years since we said, "I do." Instead, I measured our time between her references to Nuru. Since that first night in the shop, she had confided in me about her marriage to him a few more times. The more it happened, the more I wondered, *Is there truth to it?*

This egregious possibility blazed through my mind just now as I stared at the ceiling in our bedroom. Georgieta and Nuru . . .

Her fingers, caressing my face, sensuously traced the lines of time, interrupting my thoughts. Turning to her, I was breathless. I touched her face. The contrast between her dark complexion and my pale hand, with long fingers and knuckles starting to knot with age, triggered a memory.

I remembered her voice from decades earlier, sharp with frustration as we'd browsed through dusty antique shops for our first home. "They're staring at us again, Jakub," she'd said, her fingers tightening around my arm. I'd looked around, seeing nothing but furniture and curious shopkeepers. "You never see what's right in front of your face," she'd laughed, but there was an edge to it, a weariness I may have dismissed too easily then. What else had I failed to see in those early days, when I was sure I'd won the only prize that mattered?

When she leaned into me, her lips soft against my neck, I forced myself back to this moment, to her touch that still made my pulse quicken after all these years. Her hands were sure, deliberate, mapping the geography of my body with the confidence of decades spent learning each other's rhythms.

"I love you," I murmured against her chunky locs as we moved together, slow and tender, her body responding to me with an intimacy that transcended memory. In this moment, she was completely present, completely mine. She was gasping my name, her fingers digging into my shoulders as pleasure built between us.

Afterward, as our breathing steadied and she curled against my chest, she pressed a sleepy kiss to my collarbone.

"*Dɔ agbe*, Nuru," she whispered in her native language, already drifting away. I had no idea what it meant, but her words landed on me like a bag of bricks from a second-story window.

My mind and body felt like they were about to collapse, but I remained perfectly still, holding her closer, refusing to let go. Her cheek pressed to the soft padding of my chest that hadn't been there when we first married, my heart thudding too fast beneath her palm. I knew what I had to do next.

Fragment IV (Day 17)

Nuru's voice still held that velvet warmth that whisked me back to carefree college nights of double dates, cheap beer, and easy laughter. Back then, we still called each other "brother" and meant it. That version of us was long gone; we'd drifted so far apart over the years that "best friend" had become a story we told other people, not ourselves.

Thinking about him now made me sick. My fingers whitened around the phone; every note of his greeting grated.

"How's Georgieta?"

"Let's meet."

"I'm in your town."

"What? You and Georgieta didn't say you were coming . . ."

"It's just me. She has appointments and is with one of her friends. I'm here only for the day."

He must have heard the edge in my voice. A beat of silence passed.

"Come down. I'm at the diner."

His tone turned somber. "Hmm. All right. Twenty minutes."

I ended the call and glanced around the cafe where Nuru and I had killed so many late-night cravings. He'd never left this sleepy town after graduation; I hung on for a few years, then followed Georgieta to Maryland.

Plenty of time. I rang her.

"My love."

"Jakub, where are you? Liz and I are at the lab. This amyloid PET-CT is supposed to tell all. I'm nervous."

"That's why Liz is there. I have to share you once in a while."

She chuckled.

"I'll see you when you get home."

"What?"

"Don't worry. Liz has enough tea to spill with you."

"But . . ."

"The person I'm meeting just walked in, love. We'll talk later, okay?"

"Okay."

A tall, broad-shouldered Black man stepped inside, surveying the room with practiced calm. A close-cut beard framed his jaw; the flash of kente inside his cufflinks caught the light as he moved. Nuru always carried home with him.

He smiled and strode over. I didn't return it. I caught my reflection in the window behind him. I bristled at my pale face, thinning sandy hair, suit jacket a little too tight across the middle these days. I hated how small I suddenly felt next to his easy, grounded presence.

I beckoned the server with a wave; they filled Nuru's mug.

"Nothing else for now," I said, cutting off any chance Nuru could order anything else. Nuru's brow lifted.

"What's going on, Jakub?"

"Georgieta has early onset Alzheimer's."

He flinched. Caught a sharp breath, his hand darting toward mine. He stopped the motion when I drew back into a fist. An awkward gulf opened between us.

"Is she all right? And you? You're shutting me out, brother."

I spat the word. "Well, brother, something surfaced in her . . . forgetfulness. She remembers being married before me."

His eyes narrowed, replaying my words.

"You said you knew Georgieta's family in Ghana. Did you know . . ."

"Jakub . . ."

"No deflections, Nuru. I want everything."

"What exactly are you asking?"

"Fuck, Nuru. She says she was married to you."

Silence. A waitress veered away.

"Were you together," I whispered, "before us?"

"It was complicated."

"Uncomplicate it. My wife recounts intimate details she shouldn't know. Unless . . ."

"Unless what?" His gaze sharpened. "What are you accusing me of, brother?"

Brother again! It was no longer a bond; just a shield.

"For once, give me the whole truth."

He chose his words. "The truth isn't always what we think. Sometimes it's better to . . ."

"To let me question every memory?" My voice grew loud. "You went after her first, didn't you? Before that conference, when I met her."

His jaw set. He swept the diner. I followed his gaze. An elderly couple by the window, a construction crew at the counter. Lowering his voice to a dangerous whisper, he said, "You really want to do this here? You expect me to sit through your public meltdown?"

A flush of heat filled my neck and cheeks. "Don't . . ."

"Don't what?" His voice remained controlled, but I could see the tension in his grip around his coffee cup, his knuckles pressing hard against the ceramic. I caught something under his breath, barely audible: "Typical. Make it about you."

"What did you say?"

"You're not ready for the truth, brother. You never were."

I leaned in, voice rising even more. "So there was something . . ."

"Keep your voice down." Heads turned. "I won't play the angry Black man in your spectacle."

Cold shame washed through me.

"You think I don't see the actual issue?" His tone was intense. "It isn't her memories. It's that a woman like Georgieta might have chosen a man like me, a Black man, an African, first."

"That's not . . ."

"Isn't it?" His smile thinned. "All these years, you've wondered why she picked the ugly spreadsheet guy with the ten-year plan. Now her mind whispers maybe she didn't."

"Stop."

"Her skin, Jakub." Each word sliced. "That's what's gnawing at you."

The diner shrank around us, every clink amplified. He rose, set a twenty on the table. Still considerate.

"You want truth? Some doors stay shut for a reason. Decide if you love your wife enough to stop owning her whole story." He buttoned his suit jacket. "And figure out whether you're fighting for her memory or just fighting to win."

He paused, pity flickering in his eyes. "Take care of her."

The bell over the door chimed as he left. My coffee cooled while unspoken accusations settled like silt.

The quiet wasn't absence; it was a crowd of things unsaid. And I had to face the possibility that Nuru was right.

I sat in that diner for another hour after he left, staring at my cold coffee while his words echoed: *You're fighting for her memory or just fighting to win.* The truth was a knife twisting in my chest. Maybe I had been trying to win, to own every piece of Georgieta's history like some prize I'd earned.

The drive home felt endless. Every mile forced me to confront what I'd become: a man so desperate to possess his wife's past that he'd forgotten to cherish her present.

When I arrived, Liz was still there, sitting at our kitchen table with a cup of tea cooling in front of her. Her dark eyes held the same worry I'd been carrying for months.

"How did it go with Nuru?" she asked, though my face probably told her everything.

I slumped into the chair across from her. "Not well. Liz, I need to ask you something, and I need you to be completely honest with me."

She nodded, waiting.

"Georgieta's memories of being married to Nuru. Is there any truth to them being together? You knew them both back home. Did something happen between them I don't know about?"

Liz glanced at the Polish cheese on the counter. Georgieta must have taken it from the fridge while I was gone. Breaking off a small piece, she examined it curiously before her expression grew serious. "Jakub, at the appointment today, she mentioned a funeral again. The prostate cancer, the marriage . . ." She looked up at me. "I think she's confusing memories, but not in the way you might think."

"What do you mean?"

She paused, carefully choosing her words. "As children, we always put Georgieta and Nuru together when playing 'house.'"

My chest tightened. "So there was something between them."

"Childhood games, Jakub. But . . ." She hesitated. "There was a Chief back home. Chief Addo. He died of prostate cancer when we were all teenagers. It was a big funeral, bringing all the village families together. The Chief's funeral was significant. There was talk, you know how it is in our culture, about destiny, about matches that were meant to be. I think her mind is taking those old memories, that childhood pairing, the Chief's death, and weaving them into something that feels real to her now."

"But they were never actually . . ."

"Married? No. But Jakub, in her heart, in those childhood dreams we all had, maybe they were." Liz reached across the table and touched my hand. "That doesn't make your marriage any less real. It just means her mind is returning to the very beginning, to the first time someone told her she belonged with Nuru."

After Liz left, I sat alone in the quiet house, processing what she'd told me. But more than that, I was processing what Nuru had forced me to confront about myself. The truth was uncomfortable.

I had spent years quietly battling insecurities I'd never admitted, wondering if I was enough for a woman like her, being on the outside of conversations she spoke with her family or Nuru, suspicious that they were saying bad things about me in her native tongue. Her imagined marriage to Nuru had awakened every buried fear. I didn't deserve her. She might have been happier with someone who shared her heritage, her struggles, her understanding of the world in ways I never could.

Yet, sitting there, I realized our home held so many years of shared memories. Photos of vacations, family, friends, and us filled every part of the walls. The antique side table held her reading glasses, near the bookshelf overflowing with years of stories, hers and mine. I found myself slowly counting the flower-patterned throw pillows strewn across the furniture until my eyelids grew heavy. I forced them open, stood up, and went to care for the version of my wife waiting for me upstairs.

Fragment V (Day 21)

A letter arrived. No return address, but I recognized Nuru's careful script immediately. Turning on the lamp on the side table allowed me to see clearly.

Inside, two photographs slipped out. I picked up the first. The picture showed Georgieta at that conference twenty-five years ago, capturing her mid-gesture during her presentation. She looked radiant in her dark brown suit, her face animated with passion as she spoke to the audience.

On the back, in Nuru's precise handwriting: "The moment I was proud to see our sister from the motherland shine, and because you chose her and she you, the moment you became my brother. Take care of my sister."

The second picture showed two families posing together. Everyone was in full traditional Ghanaian attire. At the center, in the front row, were young Nuru and Georgieta, perhaps as teenagers. On the back of this photo was the inscription: "The Mensah and Addy families at Chief Addo's funeral. The Chief was the one who always said these two would marry."

I stared at the photographs for a long time, studying her face in both. They were so young in the family photo, so brilliant and accomplished at the conference. It hardly mattered anymore whether Georgieta pulled her fragmented memories from real childhood dreams or created entirely new narratives. What mattered was the woman upstairs, humming off-key as she arranged flowers she'd forgotten she'd bought the day before.

"Jakub?" She appeared in the doorway, hesitant. I could tell by the way she held herself, slightly uncertain, searching my face for recognition, that she was deep in one of her alternate realities again.

"Yes, my love?"

"I was thinking about Nuru today." Her voice was soft, vulnerable. "Do you think he's at peace now that he's passed?"

The question might have destroyed me once. *She speaks of our very much alive friend as if he were dead.* Now I simply nodded, understanding that in her reconstructed reality, the Chief's death had become Nuru's death. "I think he's at peace, Georgieta. I think he knows he was loved."

She smiled then, relief washing over her features. "Good. I would hate for him to have died thinking otherwise."

I opened my arms, and she settled against me on the couch, her head finding its familiar place on my shoulder. Through the window, I could see the dogwood trees beginning to shed their blossoms, petals drifting like snow across our yard.

"Tell me about him," I said quietly. "Tell me about Nuru."

She looked up at me, surprised. "You want to hear?"

"I want to hear everything you remember."

So she told me about wedding bells that may have never rung, about a honeymoon in Cape Coast that might have existed only in her mind, about quiet Sunday mornings and shared laughter that felt real enough to ache. She spoke with such tenderness, such love, that I found myself mourning this phantom marriage alongside her.

When she finished, she traced patterns on my chest with her fingertip. "He would have liked you, I think. You're both good men."

"*Nye dzi*," I whispered, remembering more Ghanaian words she'd spoken in her sleep months ago. "What does that mean?"

Her eyes lit up. "My heart. It means 'my heart' in Ewe." She pressed her palm against my chest. "You are nye dzi, Jakub. You always have been."

I kissed the top of her head, breathing in the familiar scent of her hair: shea butter and sweet almond oil, with hints of coconut and clove from the oil she twisted into her locs that morning.

"Let's go see a play tomorrow at the playhouse."

"Yes! And we must get Italian after," she said. I rolled my eyes, and she giggled.

She fell asleep in my arms as the sun set, her breathing even and peaceful.

In the morning, she might remember being married to Nuru again, or she might wake up knowing only me. Either way, I would be there, ready to step into whatever role her mind had written for me.

Stay

— ♥ —

She read the email twice. The first time it barely made sense; the second time it made too much.

"As part of standard vendor diligence, we located documentation regarding your 2019 complaint at Clarion Systems. In light of this, we will pause onboarding until Legal reviews your suitability for an enterprise role requiring discretion and alignment."

Ari Parker closed her laptop in the client's lobby. Terrazzo, wet shine, her calves and blazer tails mirrored back at her, a security guard's curious glance skimming the surface. She slid the machine into her bag, breathed, and let the words settle where they always did, in that sore place between her ribs and her throat where the body stores the memory of being called "trouble."

She'd flown into Chicago last night to start the turnaround on Monday. Process triage, change management: she did the work that other people feared. She could cool a room with a sentence and map pathways out of chaos with one whiteboard marker. She could read the yeses, the maybes, the unspoken no's, and get executives to sit up straighter while the hands-on folks believed the suits might finally be listening. She had built a life out of it, along with a reputation and now, a paper trail.

Back in 2019, she'd been younger and less practiced at smiling through other people's discomfort. Clarion had hired her to certify its diversity audit. She wouldn't rubber-stamp number magic, the opportunistic promotions three days before quarter's end, the exit packages that bought silence. When she filed the internal complaint, a VP patted her forearm as if she were a niece with a wild idea, then told Legal she was "combative." Her name entered the minutes, and when the thing leaked, it entered the backroom executive business press. Years later, the language still circled back: pause, review, discretion, alignment. As if she hadn't been aligned with the truth all along.

Her phone buzzed. She knew the energy before the name.

Come outside, Langston's text said. He always opened with a directive, but on her it sounded like an invitation.

Late spring heat lifted off the sidewalk in visible waves. He leaned against a car he had no business renting, arms crossed at the wrists, a white tee soft on his chest, as if it had known him for years. Handsome that made strangers look once, then again. Handsome that woke Ari faster than coffee.

"How did you . . ."

"You posted a photo from O'Hare, Ms. 'No Location Tags.' I did a little math. You know I'm not above showing up."

"I know," she said, trying not to smile and failing. "You also know I have a kickoff. Or had."

He watched her the way a man watches a flame he wants to coax bigger. "Let it wait."

"I can't let it wait."

He stepped closer, his voice dropping until it was a low vibration she felt in her sternum. "Let it wait for brunch," he urged. "Come with me. Eat real food, let's chill all afternoon, and leave the laptop shut."

"Your suggestion and your intention are both suspect," she replied, but her body was already relenting. She'd endured a three-hour delay and survived on airport almonds; she was done. In the eyes of procurement, she was just a high-risk algorithm flag, and to the humans in charge, she was a problem not worth their time.

Also, Langston had a way of making the clock irrelevant. He had a way of making everything immediate. The last time they hooked up, he served her beef short ribs he'd braised all night. Then, as a needle settled into the groove of a jazz record to undress to, he breathed a tune into the curve of her neck.

Today, his eyes, his smile, and his open arms promised a distraction that would immediately mute her hurt.

"At least let me drive you to the hotel," he said.

Yes, please heal me of the hurt at being cast aside by this client. Make me forget the loss of the assignment I was very much looking forward to.

She stepped inside when he opened the car door to the smells of citrus, leather: his signature scent. Soon, Chicago's riot of mid-rise glass and old stone slid by. When her phone buzzed again, he kept his eyes on the road.

"You want me to ignore that for you?"

"I know how to ignore things," she said. "I'm choosing not to. This is the client. Or the almost-client."

"Ari." Her name flowed like marshmallow dipped in chocolate syrup from his lips. So sweet the sound, she almost did not attend to the words that followed.

"You can't invoice a burnt-out woman back to life."

"And yet," she said, "burnout pays well in this economy."

He laughed, and she wanted to crawl inside the sound and make a home. For now, she turned away from him and answered.

Empty words were exchanged. *Appreciate. Unfortunate. Hope you understand.* When she hung up, she let her head rest against the seat and closed her eyes.

"Come to my place. I have a few ideas on how to get your mind off the city and onto something much more interesting."

She went. She always went to Langston the way a body seeks shade: automatic, necessary, temporary.

While he moved around the kitchen with the attention of someone who understood feeding people as a form of argument, she noticed the books stacked on his counter: sauce-stained cookbooks, a collection of Langston Hughes (of course), and Baldwin's *The Fire Next Time.*

She picked that one up and fanned the pages. She raised one eyebrow at a receipt for a fire pit purchase, which marked page 47. Langston had highlighted the lines which read, "If the concept of God has any validity or any use, it can only be to make us larger, freer, and more loving. If God cannot do this, then it is time we got rid of Him." She quickly closed the book and noticed its spine was cracked in three places, like he'd argued with it and come back for more.

He fed her in small, exact portions. Her shoulders unclenched. After, she slept on his couch while he took a few calls and pretended not to watch her breathe like a man rediscovering the pleasure of company.

By evening, she'd drafted a response to the client. In professional words, she said she wouldn't be rewritten by anyone's fear. Her name was on that complaint because she put it there. She could sign an NDA about her work and still keep her integrity. She sent it. Before the what-ifs took root, another message arrived from an international number she hadn't memorized but already knew.

EZRA: "If you're still in Chicago, call me when you can. If you're in Toronto next week, I can make time for you. Also, sunny here, but you know I prefer overcast. Don't laugh."

***

Ezra lived a few miles from the airport she landed in when work took her to the Greater Toronto Area: rows of brick, quiet streets, basketball nets over garages, a grocery where aunties slipped her extra herbs because her eyes reminded them of nieces they missed.

He was a Black man from Baltimore carrying America in his posture, even when the postal code said otherwise. He designed public spaces where people felt held: libraries, community centers; and he had the composure of someone who respected measuring tapes. He laughed easily, but rarely at people. In Ari's private taxonomy, he was a soothing place to lean.

They'd met at a client dinner. Ezra, consulting on an innovation hub, had looked at her and asked not what she did, but what she kept.

She'd said, her grandmother's recipe for stewed chicken, a silver letter opener that didn't open letters so much as remind her they once existed, and the habit of calling joy by its name even in rooms where joy looked like a misprint. He'd said, his father's ring in a velvet bag in his desk, a scarf worn too much because it still held his sister's hair oil, and long morning walks. Then coffees, then lunches, then a lake weekend passing a paper cup of fries back and forth, saying almost nothing except yes to gulls and no to work.

Ezra wished for her unhurried days. "You don't owe the calendar a tithe," he said once, stirring honey into tea with a surgeon's focus. "What if success looked like afternoons swaying in a hammock?"

"You sound like a brochure," she'd said, but the corner of her mouth had betrayed her. He talked about building a life that wasn't an emergency. A deck he wanted to make with his own hands. It would be a place where a person could read a paperback and let the sun take its time. Rest required design, he said, same as a building. Same as a good apology.

***

On the plane east, she thought about both men and how their names fit in her mouth differently. When she landed, she texted Ezra before the gate. "I'm in town. Lunch? Another client paused me for the same old reason. I'm tired of being a tab someone opens and closes."

He replied. "Lunch, yes, if you want a lawyer to help correct that search result, I know someone. We can eat first. Or skip food and walk."

They walked. His neighborhood kept its own rhythm: a barbershop with *Maze, Featuring Frankie Beverly* playing low, a Trini spot that knew the right hour for *doubles*. When they arrived back at his place, they lingered outside, and Ari talked until she was done. Ezra stood with his hands in his pockets, as if he was holding himself in place so he wouldn't move toward her too fast.

"You can build a wall, paint your name on it, and let other people crash against it," he said. "You can also build a bench with your name inscribed on the backrest, sit and engage in conversation with others. Either way, it's your name."

Something in her loosened. "You and your metaphors."

"I'm a philosopher at heart," he said, smiling. "Also, I brought you something."

It was a small box. Inside, a brass plate like the kind affixed to handcrafted shelves, engraved with her full name and her birth year. The plate sat in her palm like a decision.

"For when you build something with your hands," he said. "Or your heart. Or both."

"Thanks," she whispered.

After a bit of silence, they moved inside.

Her gaze drifted across his living room: a drafting table by the window, plants that actually looked spoken to, a shelf where *Parable of the Sower* leaned against architecture texts and a worn copy of *A Pattern Language.*

Ari pulled the Octavia Butler book. Its margins were dense with penciled notes, as if he'd been in a long conversation. Later, over soup and thick-crusted bread, he asked if she could imagine scaling life back just enough that her nervous system could stay in the room. "I don't want to watch you be great at disappearing," he said. "I want to watch you be great at staying."

"Staying where?" she asked, though she knew it was the wrong question. She could see herself in a row house with a small patch of grass, a plant she didn't forget to water, and a kitchen that forgave late-night toast. She also craved a bed so warm the morning spun around it, a city where buildings leaned into each other like kin, arms to disappear into for an hour that felt like the longest day in June.

Between those, she kept trying to build what got knocked loose every time a risk team pulled up the tiny moment of her story: a life that made room for all of her, even the inconvenient parts.

***

Still in Toronto that Friday, she checked out a leadership symposium at her hotel after seeing a LinkedIn ad. The banner read *Women Who Stayed the Course.* The keynote speaker, Dr. Ruth Okafor, stood onstage in a red sheath dress and looked as if she could thrive in any boardroom. Her stance declared, *Authority is here.*

"I used to think integrity meant never bending," Dr. Okafor said. "Then I learned some truths need time before they can be heard. Some doors open slower than justice would like." Those words hit a nerve, reminding her exactly of the email her client had sent earlier.

The speaker spoke about a scandal thirteen years earlier: refusing to falsify data, how the firm buried her, how the reforms she'd fought for arrived two years later with someone else's name stapled on top. "You won't always get the credit," she said. "But you will get the mirror. You need to be able to stand there."

In the Q&A, someone asked if she ever regretted speaking up. "No," Dr. Okafor said. "I regret believing everyone else had to be the villain for me to be right. I learned that institutions don't change because of righteous accusers. They change from persistence."

Afterward, Ari lingered in the lobby pretending to scroll. When Dr. Okafor walked by, Ari quietly thanked her. "I've been called combative," she admitted.

"That just means they heard you before they were ready to listen," Dr. Okafor said. "The trick is deciding whether to stay until they are."

Back in her hotel room, Ari replayed the words. Righteousness had been her armor and her elevation. She was right to file that complaint. She was also wrong to believe that being right exempted her from compromise. Both could be true. Maybe integrity wasn't a weapon or a shield. Perhaps it was a muscle. I could learn when to flex. I could understand when to rest.

She flew back to Chicago.

***

The following week, Legal called from the client to say they'd proceed with onboarding if she signed an extra clause. Two careful paragraphs asked her to stipulate that the 2019 complaint did not reflect her current beliefs about "appropriate collaboration." The old sore place flared. She sent the clause to Ezra and to Langston.

Langston replied first. He texted a photo of his forearm, where the dark ink rose like heat along a vein. The tattoo depicted dandelion fluff transforming midair into a silhouette of birds in flight, a stark contrast to the screen's glow. The message followed: *nah. no clause. no leash. come here.*

Ezra took longer. He'd called the lawyer he knew. His text came with a screenshot and a few words circled. "Ask them to replace 'beliefs' with 'actions.' Say: I collaborate in ways that honor values and people. That hasn't changed. That won't change."

She drafted her response and hovered. Then she closed the email and opened a new document. The words began as a letter to the person at Clarion who had first typed "combative" into the minutes. By the second paragraph, it was an account of what she'd seen, what she'd done, and who she'd tried to be. She wrote it for herself. "There is a difference between privacy and silence," she typed.

I decide where my story ends, she thought. When she finished, she didn't send it. She saved it under a name only she would recognize and closed the lid like tucking a child into bed.

Evening pressed close. On the narrow balcony of her rental, the sky tried on pink, then gold. Her phone lay on the table between a glass of water and the brass plate. In her notebook app, she drew a small rectangle, then another, and wrote beside them: bench or wall. She tapped the rectangle where the bench might be. She added a third shape and labeled it "door."

She took a deep breath in and out, and felt something inside relax. She opened her recent calls and looked at the two names she could reach with a tap. It would be easy to go to Langston, to be reckless on purpose, to let urgency teach her body a new definition of rest. It would be easy to go to Ezra, to sit with tea while he measured the angle of her smile and adjusted the room. Both wanted softness for her. Both wanted to keep the current from snatching her away, one by turning downstream, one by lifting her to the bank.

She typed two texts, one to each of them, but she didn't send them. She decided on something else. She opened her calendar, blocked the next three days, and titled the block: *"Stay."*

The next morning, she went to the downtown office and sat at a long table with people whose haircuts cost more than rent. She laughed when the CFO made a joke, gently corrected someone's misuse of the word "mitigate," and placed three sticky notes where everyone could see them: "listen, learn, change." When Legal slid the revised clause across the table, "beliefs" replaced with "actions," she read it once and signed her name as if she meant it.

***

At lunch, she walked to a small square where a fountain gurgled greenish water from its spout, and a child in a red jacket splashed the pool. At a practical distance, she sat on the edge and took out her phone. Sunlight hit the glass, and her reflection looked back at her, mouth softened, shoulders level. She pulled the brass plate from her pocket, its weight warm in her hand. She opened the unsent drafts to Langston and to Ezra. She looked at each one long enough to feel what they offered. Then she deleted them both.

For once, there was no one to perform calm for. No inbox to watch. No voice to reach for to settle the nerves under her ribs. She powered the phone down and slipped it beside the plate.

The afternoon thinned into evening. Water rose and fell, keeping its own time. Ari stood and walked without a destination, past a hardware store where she could ask how to mount a name on something not yet built, past a café where the barista drew hearts over the customer names, past the glass facades that held the city together. She thought about walls that protect and walls that imprison, and the trick of knowing which she had built. She thought about benches and doors.

She was still combative, becoming kind, and learning when and how to apply each. For the first time in years, she was also alone, by choice and at peace, her name weighty in her pocket, the night ahead wide enough to hold it.

Stay

Love In Cosmic Times ...
Again

— ♥ —

Twenty years after falling in love with a lie, Tessa Reyes had rebuilt herself into something sharp enough to cut through any deception. Her reflection in the biometric scanner confirmed her: short silver-streaked curls, a hard jaw, warm bronze skin, and those amber eyes that now looked through people instead of at them. The machine chimed to verify her identity and authorize her access, matching the impenetrable fortress she had built around her heart.

The scanner flashed blue against her palm. She didn't flinch.

She stepped into TruthScope International's cold hallway, blazer crisp, slacks pressed, flats silent on the polished floor. Her shoulders were tight, as always. The structured clothing helped her hide the softening in her midsection, the small betrayals of time, but nothing could hide the scar through her left eyebrow. She touched it once; an unconscious gesture she immediately stopped.

"Morning, Ghost Hunter," Detective Santos called from across the bullpen. He lounged in his chair, the opposite of her rigid efficiency. "New ghost network case for you. Want to bet this one's impossible like the last sixteen?"

Tessa placed her messenger bag on her desk with practiced precision. "I don't bet against impossibility," she said, voice low and rasped from years of coffee and late nights. "Show me the data."

Santos grinned at her clipped cadence. "You're tense today."

"I'm working," she replied.

That was the only answer he'd get.

She woke at 4:52 a.m. as she always did, swam her laps, drank the same bitter coffee, and checked her apartment's exits three times before leaving. There was comfort in routine; routine kept ghosts out. Or, it used to.

Once, before scanners and safeguards, there had been someone who learned her rhythms. His attention felt rare. In their calls, he noticed her breath change before her voice did. He responded to messages with such care she mistook attunement for truth. In that fractured season, being known felt like solid ground. She learned later that being known is not the same thing as knowing. Since then, she trusted systems. Systems required proof.

A voice message from Director Kim chirped overhead, synthetic optimism grating on her nerves. "Ghost identities hit another eleven corporations this quarter," he said. "Someone's slipping through authentication tiers like they're made of paper. Be vigilant."

Tessa opened the file. Screens lit her face in cool white. Her fingers hovered, then began their familiar rhythm: tap, extract, evaluate. She processed data like other people breathed.

Digital footprints everywhere. Every liar leaves one.

Patterns emerged fast. Too fast. Most reconstruction jobs fell apart under scrutiny. These didn't. Someone embedded intimate inconsistencies inside the forged identities: distinctive sleep rhythms, old injuries described in the first person, favorite foods no algorithm would randomly assign.

No amateur could do this.

And no corporate fraud lab would bother.

She was grinding her molars the way she always did when she analyzed something.

She swiped to the next case file. A jumper named David Lee had left a note, half tragic, half absurd: "If I vanish and the new me likes terrible neo-jazz fusion, just bury me twice. I curated my playlist for eight years."

The message referenced someone called The Mirror.

Tessa's fingers froze. Dark circles beneath her eyes pulsed from the strain.

The Mirror.

Her breath didn't hitch. It constricted, narrow and sharp, a fist inside her ribs. Her heart rate rose precipitously.

Santos leaned over his desk. "You good?"

"This can't be a coincidence," she whispered, not in answer to Santos, but to herself. Because of the attention to detail, the psychological nuance, the way these constructions felt human . . .

She knew that signature.

It belonged to the boy who once built her the perfect astronaut.

She stopped tapping her desk and stilled her entire body.

Three feet of personal space around her might as well have become a perimeter fence.

If this was him, she was no longer hunting a fraudster.

She was about to reopen the only wound she'd never been able to trace, classify, or cauterize.

And for the first time in years, Tessa Reyes confronted something she did not have an algorithm for.

***

Six hours later, after fielding walk-ins, calming a panicked client, wrestling two legacy systems back from the dead, and surviving on the two mints she found in the bottom of her blazer pocket, Tessa Reyes finally got the message she'd been waiting for.

The reflection shows us who we truly are.

But sometimes we need a new mirror to see clearly.

The message made her pause.

The writing style slid straight under her ribs. Philosophical but grounded. Poetic, but exact. A rhythm she hadn't seen in twenty years, yet recognized instantly.

Wright's cadence.

Or rather, Sheldon's.

Her jaw tightened. Her pulse slowed. She refused to show him panic.

The coordinates attached to the message led to an industrial recycling sector on the city's edge, where atmospheric processors droned like slow machinery breathing. She moved through the shadows with a predator's meticulousness, posture straight, shoulders locked and her flats silent on the concrete. She slipped behind a carbon filter tower, letting her eyes adjust.

A figure emerged, movement fluid, adaptive layers shifting with the dim light. He was a man of mixed heritage, racial ambiguity engineered through clothing and posture. Someone who had learned to rearrange himself to survive.

215

The Mirror. Sheldon Reynolds.

He stepped into a shaft of sickly yellow light.

"You can come out now, Detective Reyes."

Her real name cracked against her chest like a tactical round.

But Tessa stepped forward. The building's authentication system automatically scanned her, logging her presence as if she were clocking in for a shift.

"Sheldon."

He turned.

The boy she remembered had disappeared long ago. What faced her now was a man: lean, deliberate, with a pressed shirt and a jacket slightly too tight across the shoulders. His stance favored his right leg. Maybe it was an old injury, controlled well. His face carried angles time had sharpened. But his eyes, those were the same. Dark, observant, soft in the places he didn't mean them to be.

She did what she always did when something inside her threatened to respond before she was ready: she assessed.

Her brain cataloged details faster than her heart could protest. She pulled on a combination of habit, training, and emotional armor that allowed her to estimate his heartbeat by breath cadence alone.

He exhaled like he had been holding breath for two decades.

"I wondered when you'd find me," he said. His voice was thick with bass, but tugged at the edges by something like fear. "I've been watching your career."

That voice startled her more than she let on.

Deep. Measured. Almost reverent.

"The tamale detail was very you," he added softly.

Tessa's brows drew together. "I wasn't sure you'd remember."

"I remember everything," he said. "It's been a problem."

It was the closest he'd come to admitting she mattered.

"Why?" she asked. "Then and now. Why?"

The word pressed out of her with more weight than she intended.

Sheldon looked away, gaze finding the atmospheric processors cycling behind them. The continuous inhale-exhale of machines made the air feel colder.

"Then?" he said, quietly. "I was a teenager. The kid who finished assignments before the teacher finished talking, but never connected with anyone."

He swallowed and continued, "My father barely glanced at me. My mother was always working. I felt . . . invisible."

He turned back to her. That look, open, stripped down, hit her with memories she'd buried beneath decades of steely resolve.

"But I didn't create Wright randomly," he continued. "I was watching you. Learning from your forum posts from Sector Seven. Those messages about wanting someone who understood dreaming bigger. You'd talk about orbital taxis, wondering what the world looked like between stops. You loved old adventure films. You wanted someone who believed in more than the ground beneath their feet."

She swallowed and drew a careful breath.

She had forgotten those lonely old posts, the ones she buried long before she hardened.

"I built Wright out of your dreams," he confessed. "A man traveling between worlds, languages, horizons, and possibilities. I didn't make him to deceive you. I made him to be everything you wanted . . . because I wasn't."

"You were stalking my online activity when you were a kid?" she snapped, the Dominican edge slicing through her restraint.

He didn't flinch. "I was young with a massive crush on someone impossibly sophisticated. You were twenty-five. Talking philosophy, interested in space travel, and living the kind of life I had never touched."

"You were fifteen!" she exclaimed.

"I know. I know. But, I thought if I constructed a persona worthy of you, maybe . . ." His voice cracked. "Turns out that's not how love works."

"You thought I was sophisticated?" she muttered with an incredulous tone.

Before he could answer, her device chimed.

Director Kim.

Requesting her location.

"Bureau backup," she said. "Minutes out."

Sheldon lifted a memory chip. A soft glow spread into the air, unfurling holographic files; testimonial after testimonial.

A transgender woman frozen in identity purgatory.

A whistleblower hunted by corporate security.

A refugee erased by corrupted verification logs.

A Black man flagged "potentially fraudulent" because his intergalactic postal code didn't match demographic expectations.

"This is what you're shutting down," Sheldon said. "Not fraud. No, a lifeline. An underground railroad for people the system refuses to see."

Another ping.

Kim's voice: "Unverified presences detected. Backup sixty seconds out."

Sheldon stepped closer, not touching her, but close enough that she felt the gravity between them shift.

"The corporations aren't victims," he said. "They profit from keeping people in cages built from data. Authentication isn't about truth. It's about control."

Warning lights strobed through the processing stacks. Tactical boots hit the ground somewhere beyond the perimeter.

"Thirty seconds," she said.

He held her gaze.

Twenty years of guilt, longing, and something unspeakable threaded between them.

"Why show me this?" she asked.

"Because I broke something in you once," he answered. "I can't undo that. But maybe I can stop you from helping them break something bigger."

Her device buzzed again.

"Fifteen seconds."

Tessa stared at the chip, then at Sheldon.

Her jaw clenched.

Her breath steadied.

She made her decision.

She disabled her tracking beacon with a flick of her finger.

Then she stepped in, violating her own three-foot rule, and pressed a fingertip to his shoulder.

Light fractured around them.

The industrial yard vanished.

They landed in the vaulted expanse of an orbital train station: glass, steel, engines rumbling like thunder, and crowds moving beneath shifting holographic signage. A world between worlds. A place built for new beginnings.

She guided him toward a quiet bench beneath a curved arch of steel and light.

Only then did she speak, her voice low, precise, and dangerous.

"Tell me about your underground railroad."

***

The memorial wall in Tessa's office displayed forty-three photos: people who hadn't survived the Intergalactic Authentication System and its quiet cruelties. Sheldon had insisted on the wall when they established the Transitional Identity Advocacy Division, tucked into what used to be a storage wing of TruthScope's Midtown tower. "We will remember why we're here," he'd said, hanging the first frame with hands that trembled more than he wanted her to notice.

Six months since that night in the recycling district, and she still felt the weight of her choice: the moment she disabled her beacon and pulled him into orbital transit instead of turning him in.

TruthScope's corporate lawyers had called the whole thing a hoax at first, muttering about interplanetary jurisdiction and unauthorized displacement, but the testimonials Sheldon provided buried every accusation. Real faces, real stories, real harm from systems engineered to exclude. Her countersuit exposed what the corporation wanted hidden: Earth's structures had modernized, but the hierarchy beneath them had not.

Not everyone survived the fallout from the widespread corruption she exposed. Director Kim was arrested, exposed as being in the pockets of several elite consortiums, and quietly manipulating verification algorithms for profit. Detective Santos retired after the new board reinstated Tessa, promoting her to help build the new division.

"I'm too old for this," he said, hugging her goodbye.

She was thinking of the old man when she heard a soft knock. Sheldon entered, sliding through the door with the ease of someone still half-expecting to be thrown out of legitimate work. The office, once an interrogation room, suited him. He always chose seats that let him see the exits.

"Forty-seven applications today," he reported, lowering himself into the chair he used to fear. "Three retaliation cases. And someone claiming their scanner only works when they use their 'white voice.'"

Tessa accepted her cup from him, her fingers brushing his for the briefest second. Even now, still electric, still careful. "It's better than expected. People can keep core identity markers while adjusting how they present to the grid."

He studied her face the way she used to profile suspects, taking in her fatigue, the faint shadows under her eyes, the disciplined calm she'd rebuilt after the upheaval. "You look good. Tired, but good."

She huffed a laugh and said, "Yesterday someone tried to list 'Professional Dream-Drifter' as their occupation. I said no, but admired the honesty. They wanted at least one anchor while shifting between selves."

Their laughter overlapped, loose in a way that would've startled their past selves. Piece by piece, they rebuilt trust, not through confessions, but through long days, shared files, and the strange joy of unforced banter.

Back then, he had been a teenager nursing an impossible crush; she had been a twenty-five-year-old woman who shut it down the second she discovered his identity and deception. That distance had been a canyon. Now, in a future where Earth's cities punctured the stratosphere and orbital taxis linked continents in minutes, that history felt like another life. They were simply two adults trading coffee and absurd verification stories.

Their laughter thinned into a peaceful quiet. Sheldon set down his empty cup. He squared his shoulders and elongated his back before he spoke again.

"There's something I need to tell you."

She recognized that tone: equal parts fear and resolve.

"I've been thinking about deleting Wright completely."

She straightened. "Why?"

"Because he was a beautiful lie that hurt someone I cared about. And because it's embarrassing. Fifteen-year-old me thought French accents meant sophistication."

Tessa looked down, spreading her fingers across her thighs the way she did when grounding herself. She inhaled once. Exhaled slowly. He watched her without rushing.

"What if I don't want you to delete it?"

He blinked, startled. "Why keep it?"

"The Wright persona was hopeful. Romantic. Someone who believed love could cross impossible distances. Maybe that version deserves to exist, even if he's incomplete."

"Dangerous philosophy for someone in identity enforcement," he murmured.

"Everything worthwhile is dangerous." She lifted her chin. "María

---

Teresa Reyes is a construction, too. We're all becoming. Sometimes who you become is who you were meant to be."

"So, we're all elaborate identity fraudsters?"

"We're all trying to become ourselves," she said. "Some take more creative routes."

He smiled, looking innocent and unguarded. He flashed this often since they'd rebuilt their lives on this side of the law. "Would you like dinner? Not as colleagues. As people deciding who they want to be, together."

Tessa set her cup aside and held his gaze. Sheldon straightened, instinctively smoothing his jacket as if preparing for judgment.

She saw him. Not Wright. Not The Mirror. Just Sheldon, thirty-five, a fully grown man trying to offer truth without hiding behind invention.

"Yes," she said.

His shoulders loosened. His breath left in a slow, quiet release.

"But there are a few terms we need to agree on."

"Anything."

"This time I need to know who I'm falling in love with. Not Wright, the astronaut, and not the Mirror, the liberator. Just you."

His jaw slackened for a beat; his gaze flicked downward before he managed, "What if you find a man less interesting than Wright? Or less impressive than The Mirror?"

"Especially then." She grinned. "And if you show up speaking French, I'm leaving."

He laughed softly. "What about Spanish? I've been practicing."

"Absolutely not. My *abuela* would rise from the grave and drag me home herself."

His smile widened. "English it is. Maybe I'll try terrible pickup lines about biometric authentication."

"Now you're speaking my language."

She rose, circling her desk until she stood in front of him, close enough to notice the faint coffee stain on his chest and the strength outlined beneath the futuristic fabric. Close enough to count the freckles across his nose she'd never seen before. When she reached for his hand, it was the first time their palms had ever met skin to skin.

"You know what's strangest?" she said softly. "I think I'm falling for the same fictional person I fell for twenty years ago. You just learned how to be him without lying."

He turned his palm upward, fingers threading with hers. "Twenty years later, and you're still teaching me about myself."

"That's what partners do."

"Partners," he echoed. "Better than 'man who broke my heart with an elaborate digital fraud.'"

"Much better branding. Considerably less dramatic."

She leaned closer. "Though drama has its place."

Outside, vehicles glided through their aerial lanes, casting soft shadows over the tower. Earth had changed: vertical cities, atmospheric shields, trans solar commuter lines; but human connection had not. The authentication economy would never be perfect. But it was becoming honest, protecting the right to evolve rather than trapping people in corporate-defined identities.

As Sheldon stood, still holding her hand, Tessa felt something inside her settle, something that had cracked decades ago. Not forgiveness alone. Recognition. The truth is that love sometimes requires looking past performance to the person beneath.

"Dinner tomorrow on Titan?" he asked, eyes bright. "Methane

seas glowing orange under Saturn's shadow?"

"Jesus, Sheldon. Not another moon."

"A real one this time," he promised, smiling. "I'll be there."

She rose on her toes and kissed him.

Soft at first, then certain as his hands slid to her waist, as if learning her in real time. His mouth moved with deliberate care, mapping who she'd become, holding nothing back. She tasted coffee, and warmth, and something she hadn't felt in twenty years: hope.

When they broke apart, breathless, she whispered, "That's my promise."

"And our promises," he murmured, forehead touching hers, "are bona fide. Because this time, we verified our hearts."

Love of My Daughter's Daughter

— ·♥· —

Her dogs keep barking at the closet. They sense me, though they cannot see. Inside that closet, cramped like the 500 square feet she calls home, is everything I left behind: faded dresses, tarnished jewelry, a box with a photo album of her childhood, and her mother's youth. Nestled among them lies a brittle note in my sharp, slanted script: *I did the best I could with what I had.*

It's strange to watch her now, years after my death. She's grown into a beautiful woman, her face carrying hints of her mother, my daughter, and that same fire in her eyes. But does she feel that fire in her heart, or did I smother it with my sharp tongue?

The day I first saw her, she was just a baby, wrapped in a yellow blanket that smelled of desperation and cheap perfume. A note from my daughter read simply, *This is your granddaughter, Aisha.* My heart cracked as I held her, though bitterness followed quickly. I thought, *Another abandoned child, another chance to fail.* Still, her tiny fingers curled around mine, softening me for a moment.

"Looks like it's just you and me now," I whispered that night as she wailed against my shoulder.

But life hardened me again. Every scrape, every tear reminded me of her mother. My anger at my daughter spilled over onto her child.

I remember when she was seven, coming home with muddy shoes and tear-streaked cheeks.

"Grandma, Tommy pushed me down and said I don't have a real family."

I wanted to tell her that family is more than blood: it's the marrow. Blood dries, bones break, but marrow keeps working quietly inside, doing its duty. But instead, I snapped. "Stop that crying. You think tears solve anything? Hold your head up. Push back. Show them you're stronger than their words."

Her shoulders squared, but the sparkle in her eyes dimmed.

By her teens, our dinners were edged with tension.

"I got accepted to the debate team," she said, glowing.

"Good. Maybe all that arguing with me will finally serve a purpose."

Her face fell. "Why can't you just say you're proud of me?"

I cleared the table saying only, "Pride comes before a fall."

That night, I stood by her door, listening to her muffled sobs.

"Grandma?" she whispered through the wood. *She knew I was there!*

"What?"

". . . Never mind. Goodnight."

I wanted to say, *"I love you."* Instead, I walked away, saying nothing.

———

***

Years later, Dr. Martinez arrived with a manila envelope. It turned out my daughter and her husband hadn't abandoned Aisha; tuberculosis had taken them. They'd left her to spare her the sight of their decline. She handed me a photograph and a teddy bear. In the photo, my daughter and her husband. They were smiling despite appearing to be physically fading. They held the teddy bear they purchased for Aisha's sixteenth birthday. Perhaps they hoped and prayed for this day, knowing it would come without them.

That evening, I called Aisha from the porch where she was reading to her room. "Sit down. I need to tell you something about your parents."

Her face went pale. "What about them?"

"They didn't abandon you, child. They loved you so much they gave you up before death could take them."

Her tears fell fast. "They loved me?"

I nodded, placing the bear on her dresser. I should have held her while she cried, but I walked away. My shame was too heavy.

***

From then on, I tried to soften, but my tongue had carved its trenches. When she left for university, she hugged me fiercely at the car.

"I'll miss you too, Grandma," she said.

"I didn't say . . ."

"I know you."

***

She rarely enters the second bedroom now—the place where she locked away the box containing me and my things. But whenever she does, her two mutts rush the door, scratching and whining with frantic certainty. *They know I am here.*

Today, she comes in for something else, yet she paused near the closet. She observes her pups, then looks at the doors, as if finally seeing the connection. At last, using both hands, she pulls open the passage that leads to me.

The air is stale with lavender. She lifts the green dress, finds the note in its pocket, and reads. Tears spill as she sinks to the floor.

The room shifts. Warmth ripples through the air. *She senses me.*

"Grandma?" she whispers. "Is that you?"

I gather everything I never said, and this time it finds her. *"I'm here, child."*

Her breath catches. "I . . . I can hear you."

"You always could, even when I couldn't speak the words."

She clutches the note. "You were hurting too. The whole time, Grandma. I knew. You were always carrying so much pain."

"I was. But that doesn't excuse how I treated you. You deserved love, softer words."

Her voice trembles. "I just wanted you to love me."

"Oh, baby girl. I did love you. Fiercely. Always. Every hug you gave me, every time you forgave me: inside my silence was love I could not return."

She sobs, but her face eases. "I wish we'd had more time. I wish you had said it, even once."

"I love you, Aisha," I whisper, wrapping her in the warmth I never

gave in life.

The dogs settle, their tails tapping softly against the floor. She closes her eyes, breathing deeply, as if held.

"It's okay now," she murmured. "I am okay."

"Yes," I say, my voice thinning like morning mist.

And for the first time, I believe it. The bitterness dissolves, leaving only peace. Maybe this is forgiveness; not hers, but mine.

"I love you, Grandma," she says into the empty room.

"I love you too, Aisha. Always did. Always will."

***

As my words fade and Aisha sits quietly among my belongings, I feel a familiar warmth behind me. I turn, and there she is, my daughter. She is radiant and whole, her face free of the gauntness that tuberculosis carved into her final days.

"Hello, Mama," she says, her voice carrying the same gentle strength I remember from her childhood.

"My baby girl." The words come easier now, unburdened by decades of pride and pain.

She takes my hand. "You did well with her, you know. She's strong because of you."

"I was so hard on her. So hard on you. Just like my mother was hard on me, and her mother before that."

My daughter's eyes fill with understanding. "Mama, now the chain has broken. Look at her: she's choosing forgiveness over bitterness. She's choosing to heal instead of hurting."

I watch Aisha clutching my note, her face peaceful despite the tears in her eyes. "She won't pass this down?"

"No, she'll remember your sacrifices, not your hardness." My daughter glances at Aisha with such pride. "Your work here is done, Mama."

Behind my daughter, a golden light grows, warm as summer afternoons when she was small.

"Come on, Mama. It's time to rest."

Together, we step into the light, my hand in hers: the way it should have been all along.

***

The fire pit in the apartment complex's courtyard hungers. Aisha feeds it everything: the green dress melting to nothing, the jewelry cracking, the faces in the album collapsing to ash. My note waits last in her hand: *I did the best I could with what I had.* When she lets it go. The paper curls, glows, then gives way. The fire swallows. The air stills, and I rise.

The End

— ∙■∙ —

Or so it seemed. Because some stories refuse to stay finished . . .

The sequel to *Love on the Fourteenth Floor* tears open what I left hanging on the fire escape. Jeffrey sees Marcia's feelings before she names them, then catches himself wanting more: more than closeness, more than loyalty, more than the borrowed hours she splits between everyone else. He starts to believe her full attention is something he deserves, even when it means resenting the space Talia occupies in her life. What follows is a reckoning: desire pressing hard against restraint, love making demands that friendship was never built to survive.

Order Now

•••

Get Love On The Fourteenth Floor - The Novella

https://scarletibisjames.com/books

Step back into the elevator. The doors are closing!

Your Exclusive Bonus Story

Step deeper into *What Grandmothers Hold* with the stepmother's untold story. Learn the truth behind Margaret's restraint. The burden she bore. The love she protected at a cost.

•••

Get Bonus Story Now

https://tinyurl.com/getastory

Thank you for choosing this book, for turning these pages, and for making space for these characters on your shelf.

Acknowledgments

This book didn't arrive alone. It came with patience, late-night talks, laughter when words clicked, and steady encouragement when they didn't. Most importantly, it came wrapped in love.

To my husband, thank you for believing in this work when I hesitated. Your time, space, grace, and faith carried me through. This book is a testament to our partnership.

I also honor the spirits of the characters who arrived unannounced, woke me early, and insisted on being heard. I'm grateful to my ancestors, both long-ago and recently departed, whose lives and choices made this work possible.

To my descendants who may one day read these words, know this: love isn't always clear at first glance. It needs patience, courage, humility, and sometimes the bravery to look again. These stories show that connection grows as we see each other more clearly, honestly, and with compassion.

And to every reader who believes love deserves a second look, thank you for being here. This book was written just for you. Even as I wrote it, I did not fully know the message it carried, only that it was meant to reach you. I hope you receive its spirit as gently and openly as it was given.

About the Author

Scarlet Ibis James is an award-winning contemporary romance author who infuses her stories with the warmth of her Trinidadian heritage and the electric energy of New York City, where she now resides. Having weathered a decade of Connecticut winters, complete with blizzards and power outages, she knows firsthand how isolation can illuminate truth.

James crafts delightfully flawed, deeply human characters who mirror her own blend of zest and introspection. Her engaging narratives explore the complexities of love, self-discovery, and life's unexpected turns, all delivered with humor, heart, and touches of magical realism.

A believer in hard-won happy endings, James writes for readers who like their romance with emotional honesty and their love stories earned rather than given.

Author Website: **https://scarletibisjames.com/**

Socials: @scarlet.ibis.james

Also by Scarlet Ibis James

Love. Legacy. Second chances.

Scarlet Ibis James writes contemporary stories about people rediscovering connection after distance: where tenderness is work, desire is honest, and hope is hard won.

If you enjoyed *Scarlet Yearnings Beyond First Glance,* you'll find more heartfelt journeys in these books →→→

Scarlet Yearnings
Stories of Love and Desire

Discover the origins of love's first spark in *Scarlet Yearnings: Stories of Love and Desire*, where the women of this universe first dared to want more . . .

Scarlet Yearnings offers an unforgettable collection of stories chronicling Black women's journeys through the landscape of love unfulfilled.

With characters as diverse as they are familiar, these twelve tales explore the universal hunger for genuine connection in a world where partners disappear, deceive, or simply cannot meet the depth of a woman's heart.

"An engaging short story collection that explores themes of love, desire, and life." — **Reedsy Discovery**

Poignant, powerful, and profoundly honest, this collection honors the complexity of desire and the dignity of women who continue to seek authentic love even when their experiences might counsel otherwise.

Black women journey through love's complicated terrain.

...

Get Scarlet Yearnings

https://scarletibisjames.com/books

Scarlet Birthright
What They Left Behind

Discover the full story of Joromi, first met in *What Grandmothers Hold* . . .

In *Scarlet Birthright*, Joromi Enoch's desire to emulate his father's respectability leads him to make a devastating choice abandoning his daughter Trisha in Trinidad while he builds a new life in America.

As Trisha grows up haunted by her father's absence and Joromi constructs a life that excludes his firstborn, both father and daughter must confront painful questions about love, responsibility, and redemption.

Foreword Clarion Reviews describes it as, *"A moving family saga, Scarlet Birthright is about fractured family relationships and the healing power of love."*

This emotionally charged narrative explores how the choices we make in pursuit of others' approval can create wounds that span generations, and whether healing those wounds requires us to reimagine what family truly means.

A Father's Choice, A Daughter's Journey

•••

Get Scarlet Birthright

https://scarletibisjames.com/books

Love in the Dark: A Holiday Romance for Grown-Ups

Last December, when a blizzard traps them in their Connecticut home two weeks before Christmas, Marissa and Gregory must decide if their marriage is worth saving before the New Year begins . . .

If you believe second chances are harder, and more beautiful, than first love, this novella is for you.

"I absolutely loved this story! Scarlet delivers a heartfelt, authentic tale of two souls rediscovering love." — N.G. Peltier, author of Sweethand.

Love in the Dark is a story about marriage after the honeymoon ends, love after the butterflies settle, and finding your way back to someone who's been beside you all along.

When the lights go out, the truth comes on.

•••

Get Love In The Dark

https://scarletibisjames.com/books

Also by Scarlet Ibis James

More Bonus Content

You made it to the end of *Beyond First Glance*, which tells me something about you. You like romance with layers. You want characters who try, stumble, regroup, and try again.

Since I know you aren't quite ready to leave these worlds behind, I've included bonus content just for you. On the following pages, please find ***Beyond First Glance: A Reader's Companion***, a guide designed to help you (and your favorite bookish friends) dive deeper into the "maintenance" of love. →→→

Beyond First Glance:
A Reader's Companion

"Love beyond first glance isn't magic, it's maintenance."

The Vibe Check: General Discussion

The "Maintenance" Philosophy: Scarlet Ibis James opens by telling us that love isn't just a spark; it's the work we do after the fire starts. Which couple in these stories do you think worked the hardest to keep their flame alive?

The Power of the "After": This collection was born because readers kept asking, "But what happened after?". Do you prefer stories that end on the "happily ever after," or do you find more beauty in the "reckoning" that comes later?

Seeing Clearly: The author suggests that true connection only happens when we see each other with "compassion and honesty". Was there a character you initially judged but grew to love once you saw them through a different lens?

Story Spotlights

Love on the Fourteenth Floor: Marcia and Talia have that "sister energy" we all crave. Marcia literally crawls on the floor like a "spy from a B-rated movie" just to check on her friend. How does their friendship act as its own kind of love story, especially when Talia is carrying the weight of her mother's illness?

Released for the Day: Nadine and her long-lost love reunite after twenty-two years. He tells her, "Love does not respect geography". Do you agree with him, or do you think the "oceans and visas" they faced were too much to overcome back then?

What Grandmothers Hold: Mary and Cecil are the ultimate "chosen" partners, raising their granddaughter Trisha while navigating a complicated relationship with their son. Cecil says he wouldn't change anything, even the heartbreak, if it meant having Mary by his side. Is this the most romantic moment in the book, or is it just the most realistic?

He Did Not Come Back: Cleolin's story is so tender and heavy. She finds a piece of paper with the "practical" code to unlock her late partner's phone—not a grand romantic gesture, but something so him. How does grief force us to "cross a line we cannot uncross" as we start to look for a new version of ourselves?

For the Soul

The Soundtrack of the City: From the "midnight waterfall" of locs to the "low chord on an old guitar" of a laugh, the author uses such sensory language. If you had to pick a song to represent the overall mood of this book, what would it be?

The Final Word: The author writes these stories for anyone who believes love deserves a "second look". What is one thing you're going to look at differently in your own life after closing this book?

— ■ —

Love is never simple, but sharing your review is—help others find this story: https://bit.ly/3PjzXWJ.